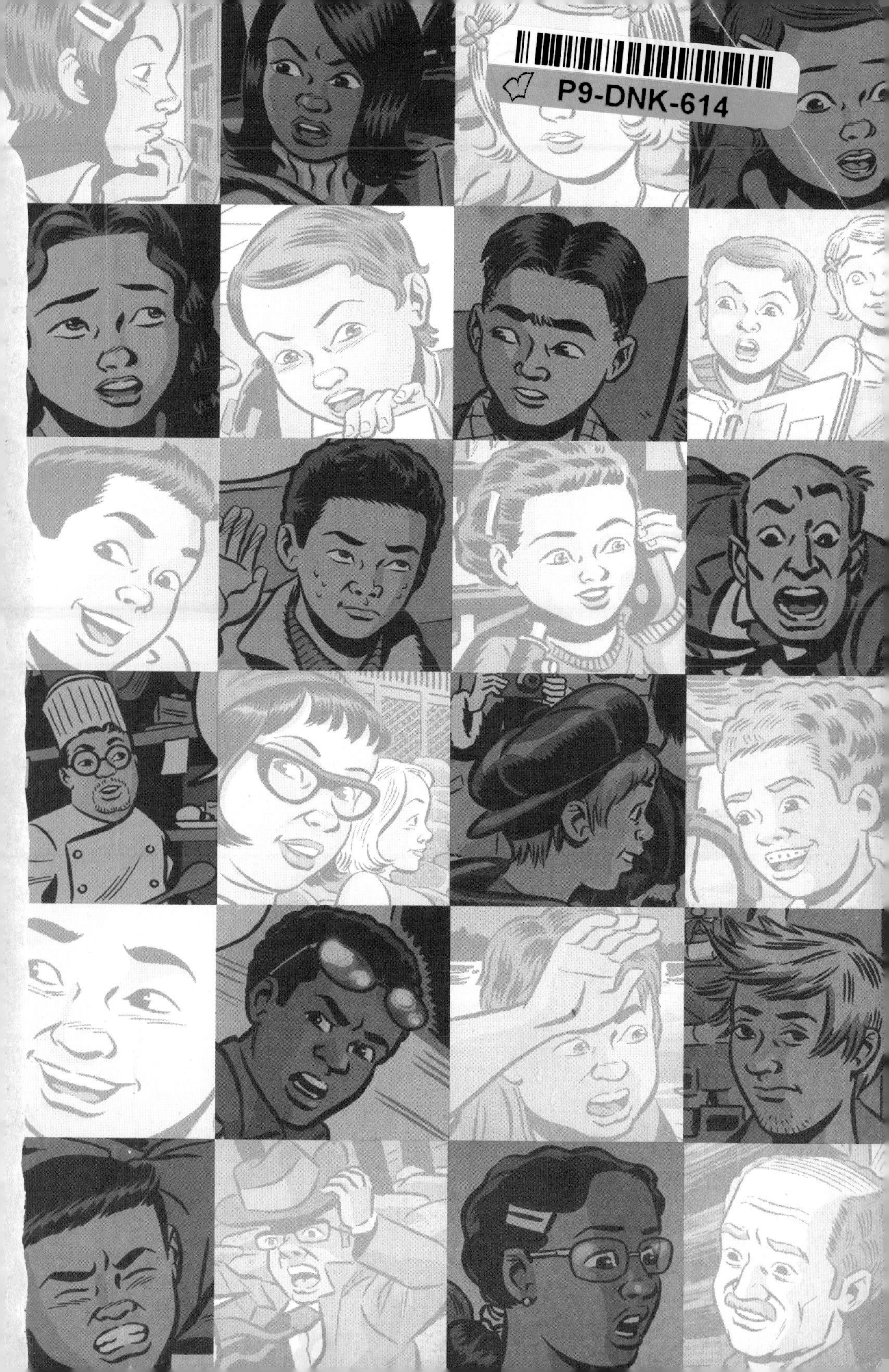

Max Finder Mystery
Collected Casebook

Volume 2

*To all Max Finder fans:
keep searching for clues and
solving mysteries.*
– LOD

2007 Bayard Canada Books Inc.

Publisher: Jennifer Canham
Editorial Director: Mary Beth Leatherdale
Assistant Editor: David Field
Production Manager: Lesley Zimic
Production Editor: Larissa Byj
Production Assistant: Kathy Ko

Design: John Lightfoot/Lightfoot Art & Design Inc.

Puzzle text: Maria Birmingham
Puzzle illustrations: John Lightfoot
Comic colouring: Peter Dawes (p. 11, 17, 23, 35, 41, 47, 53, 59, 65); Chris Stone (p. 29)
Photos: Deb Yea (p. 58; skateboard courtesy of So Hip It Hurts)

Special thanks to Angela Keenlyside, Barb Kelly, Craig Battle, and
Kim Verhaverbeke (Ashley Oaks Public School).

We gratefully acknowledge the financial support of the Government of Canada through
the Book Publishing Industry Development Program (BPIDP) for our publishing activities.

Conseil des Arts   Canada Council
du Canada   for the Arts

Library and Archives Canada Cataloguing in Publication

O'Donnell, Liam, 1970-

    Max Finder mystery : collected casebook / Liam O'Donnell, Michael Cho.

ISBN 2-89579-116-3 (vol. 1).
ISBN 978-2-89579-121-8 (vol. 2)

    I. Cho, Michael II. Title.

PN6733.036M38 2006   jC741.5'971   C2006-903300-5

Printed in Canada

Owlkids Publishing
10 Lower Spadina Ave., Suite 400
Toronto, Ontario M5V 2Z2
Ph: 416-340-2700
Fax: 416-340-9769

From the publisher of

chirp   chickaDEE   OWL

Visit us online!
www.owlkids.com

Volume 2

Liam O'Donnell

Michael Cho

Owl
kids

Max Finder
MYSTERY
Collected Casebook

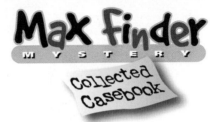

Contents

Cases

Contents

Puzzles

Extra Stuff

Collected Casebook - Volume 2

HEY MYSTERY FANS!

Welcome to the **Max Finder Mystery Collected Casebook, Volume 2!** Alison and I are really excited to bring you ten of the best mysteries to hit our hometown of Whispering Meadows.

From the **Trail Trap** to the **Summer Sinker**, each mysterious comic is crammed with clues, stuffed with suspects, and riddled with enough red herrings to keep you guessing until the last panel. We've done all the legwork, but solving the mystery is up to you! Read the mysteries, follow the clues, and try to crack the case. All the solutions are in the back of the book. But remember: real detectives never peek.

So, fire up your mystery radar and get solving!

Max

P.S. Check out the BONUS puzzles and the artist's sketchbook, too!

Trail Trap

The Case of the Trail Trap

Did you know the antpitta bird barks instead of sings? Max Finder here, fact collector and Grade 7 detective. It's a sunny autumn Sunday, and Alison and I are trekking through Warbler Woods on our latest case. The girl leading the way is Andrea Palgrave, our school's newest student and our newest client.

LESLIE CHANG TOLD ME YOU GUYS ARE THE SCHOOL'S BEST DETECTIVES, SO I FIGURED YOU COULD HELP ME OUT.

SCHOOL'S BEST DETECTIVES? WORLD'S GREATEST DETECTIVES IS MORE LIKE IT.

Andrea is a star cross-country runner. She was out for her morning run when she stepped into a covered pit in the middle of the trail. The pit wasn't there yesterday and it certainly wasn't an accident.

I COULD HAVE TWISTED MY ANKLE AND NOT BEEN ABLE TO COMPETE IN NEXT WEEK'S RUNNING MEET.

THAT WAS THE IDEA. SOMEONE WANTS YOU OUT OF THAT RACE, ANDREA.

THERE ARE LOTS OF FOOTPRINTS AND SOME PRINTS FROM A LARGE ANIMAL.

WHAT'S WITH ALL THE YELLOW TAPE?

THE TAPE IS MINE. THE ANIMAL PRINTS BELONG TO A HORSE.

The kid is Andrea's little sister, Zoe. She wants to be a crime scene investigator like her mom, and even has a lab in her basement. When Zoe heard about the trap, she rushed to the woods to collect evidence.

MY PLASTER MOULD OF THE TRAP-SETTER'S FOOTPRINT IS DRY.

HEY, ZOE. GOOD TO HAVE YOU ON BOARD.

The footprint was made by a hiking boot with a wavy tread. If we can find a boot with a matching tread, we just might find the trap-setter.

12

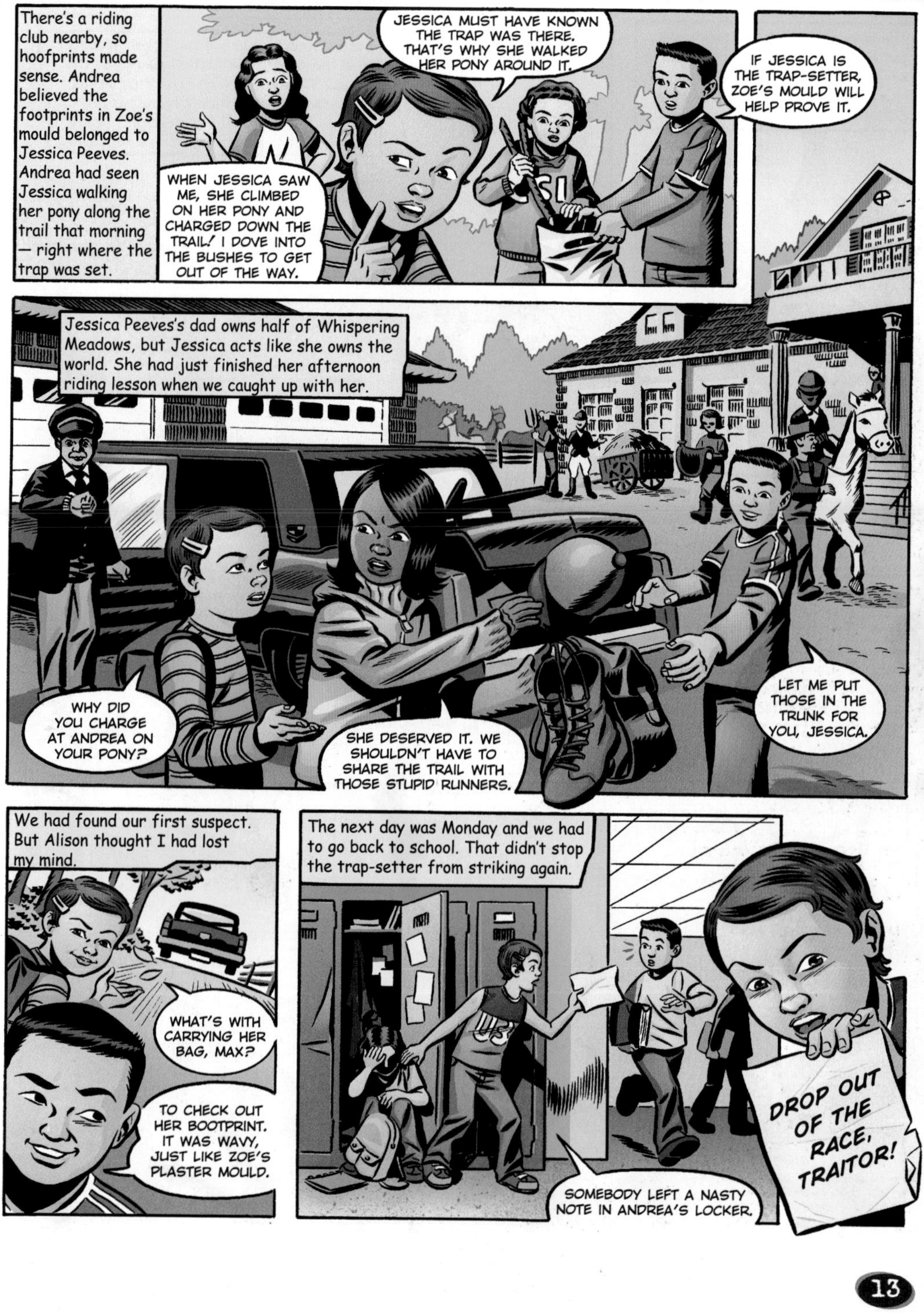
There's a riding club nearby, so hoofprints made sense. Andrea believed the footprints in Zoe's mould belonged to Jessica Peeves. Andrea had seen Jessica walking her pony along the trail that morning — right where the trap was set.
WHEN JESSICA SAW ME, SHE CLIMBED ON HER PONY AND CHARGED DOWN THE TRAIL! I DOVE INTO THE BUSHES TO GET OUT OF THE WAY.
JESSICA MUST HAVE KNOWN THE TRAP WAS THERE. THAT'S WHY SHE WALKED HER PONY AROUND IT.
IF JESSICA IS THE TRAP-SETTER, ZOE'S MOULD WILL HELP PROVE IT.
Jessica Peeves's dad owns half of Whispering Meadows, but Jessica acts like she owns the world. She had just finished her afternoon riding lesson when we caught up with her.
WHY DID YOU CHARGE AT ANDREA ON YOUR PONY?
SHE DESERVED IT. WE SHOULDN'T HAVE TO SHARE THE TRAIL WITH THOSE STUPID RUNNERS.
LET ME PUT THOSE IN THE TRUNK FOR YOU, JESSICA.
We had found our first suspect. But Alison thought I had lost my mind.
WHAT'S WITH CARRYING HER BAG, MAX?
TO CHECK OUT HER BOOTPRINT. IT WAS WAVY, JUST LIKE ZOE'S PLASTER MOULD.
The next day was Monday and we had to go back to school. That didn't stop the trap-setter from striking again.
SOMEBODY LEFT A NASTY NOTE IN ANDREA'S LOCKER.
DROP OUT OF THE RACE, TRAITOR!

The note stirred up bad memories for Andrea. When she left Twindale, her old school, Andrea's old running buddy, a girl called Shawna Carver, called Andrea a traitor.

I DIDN'T TELL ANYONE EXCEPT ETHAN. HE'S MY NEW RUNNING BUDDY AND I KNEW HE'D UNDERSTAND.

Before Andrea was around, Ethan Webster held the record for fastest runner at the school. We went looking for Ethan on the basketball court, but only found his best friend, Josh Spodek. Josh couldn't figure out why Ethan was being so nice to Andrea.

ETHAN IS AFRAID SHE'LL BEAT HIS RECORD IN THIS WEEKEND'S RACE. HE WAS JUST COMPLAINING ABOUT HER YESTERDAY DURING OUR MORNING BASKETBALL GAME.

When Ethan arrived, he was more concerned with Andrea's health than with his title as best runner at school.

ANDREA AND I USUALLY RUN IN THE MORNING, BUT I WASN'T FEELING WELL YESTERDAY. YOU GUYS HAVE TO FIND THAT TRAP-SETTER BEFORE ANDREA GETS HURT.

THANKS FOR LENDING ME YOUR SWISS ARMY KNIFE.

OKAY MR. SHOE-SNOOPER, DOES ETHAN HAVE WAVY TREADS?

NOPE. CHUNKY. DOESN'T MATCH ZOE'S PLASTER MOULD.

Andrea gave us Shawna's phone number and we called her. She denied sending the note, but agreed to talk to us anyway. We met her at Twindale.

TWINDALE PUBLIC SCHOOL

I DIDN'T SET ANY TRAPS, BUT THAT'S NOT A BAD IDEA. WITH ANDREA OUT OF THE RACE, IT'LL BE EASIER FOR ME TO WIN.

SHOE-SNOOP SURVEY SAYS WAVY TREAD! THAT MATCHES ZOE'S MOULD. SHAWNA COULD HAVE BEEN AT THE TRAIL.

OKAY, BUT HOW DID SHE HIDE THE NOTE IN ANDREA'S LOCKER?

When we got back from Twindale, the phone was ringing. It was Zoe. She'd been examining the crime scene evidence in her lab.

REMEMBER THE STICKS THAT COVERED THE TRAP? THEY WERE CUT NEATLY WITH A SMALL SAW.

INTERESTING. THANKS, ZOE.

MAX, WHAT DOES THAT KNIFE HAVE TO DO WITH OUR TRAP-SETTER?

EVERYTHING, ALISON. ABSOLUTELY EVERYTHING.

Do you know who tried to trip Andrea? All the clues are here. Turn to page 74 for the solution.

15

Square Search

Test your sleuthing smarts and find each name hidden in these blocks.

Move from letter to letter by going up, down, across, or diagonally. You can return to a letter more than once. You may not need to use every letter in each block.

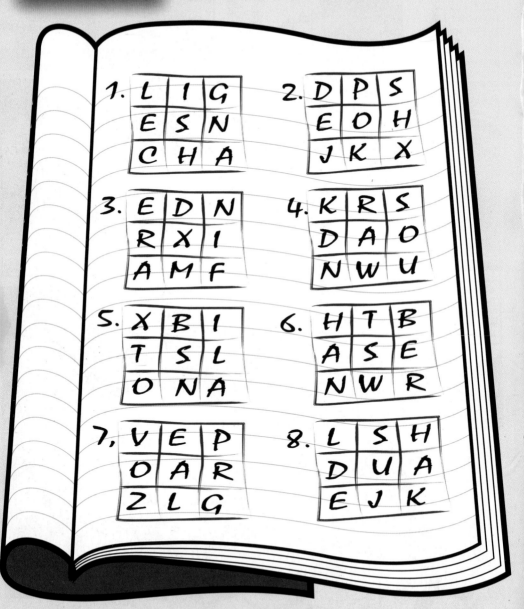

1.
L	I	G
E	S	N
C	H	A

2.
D	P	S
E	O	H
J	K	X

3.
E	D	N
R	X	I
A	M	F

4.
K	R	S
D	A	O
N	W	U

5.
X	B	I
T	S	L
O	N	A

6.
H	T	B
A	S	E
N	W	R

7.
V	E	P
O	A	R
Z	L	G

8.
L	S	H
D	U	A
E	J	K

HINT: Eight of the ten following characters' names can be found in the blocks:
Alison Santos, Josh Spodek, Ethan Webster, Nanda Kanwar, Zoe Palgrave, Leslie Chang, Lukas Hajduk, Jessica Peeves, Andrea Palgrave, and Max Finder.

ANSWER PAGE 82

The Case of the...

Model Plane Mess-up

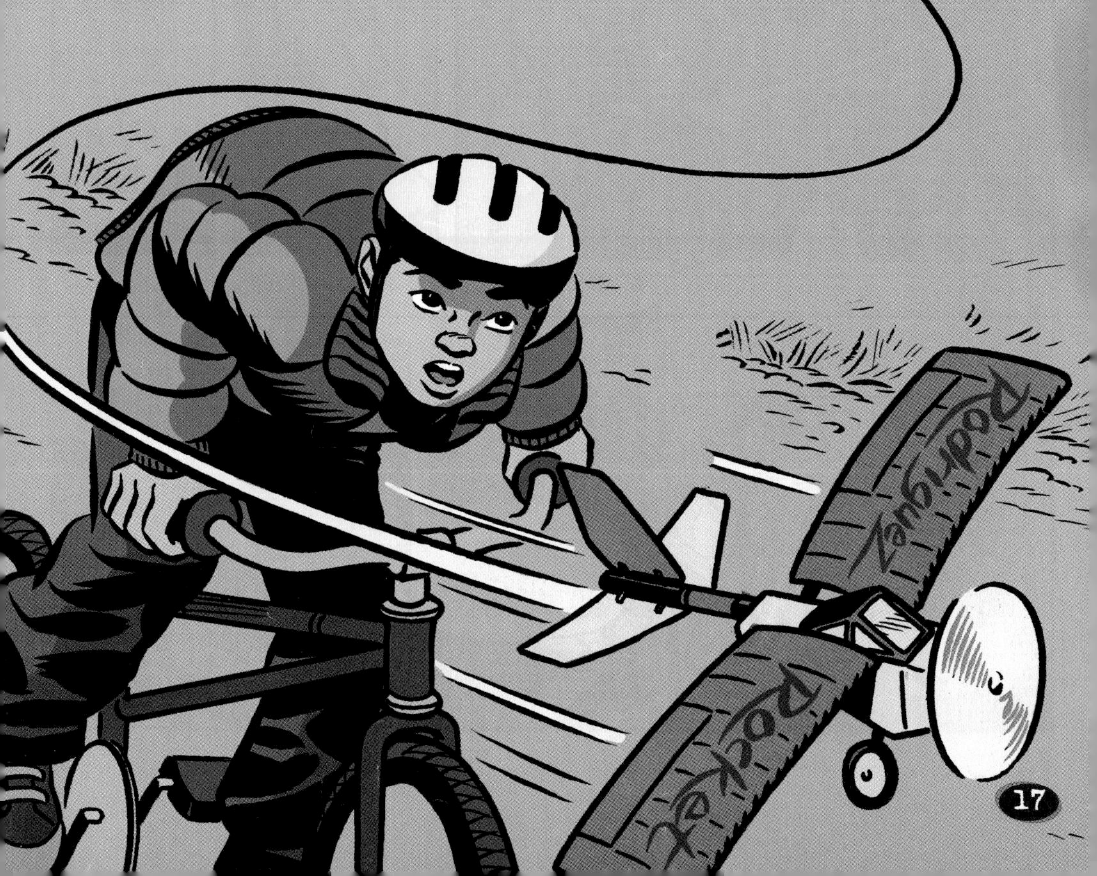
Rodriguez
Rocket

The Case of the
Model Plane Mess-up

Did you know bats are the only mammals that can fly? Max Finder here, fact collector and Grade 7 detective. It's a cool November afternoon here in Whispering Meadows. Alison and I are out for one last bike ride before the snow arrives. But, it looks like a chill isn't the only thing in the air.

WATCH OUT, MAX!

SOMETHING'S WRONG. I CAN'T CONTROL MY PLANE!

Alex Rodriguez is president of the Flying Aces model plane club. Every Saturday, the club takes over Oakdale field. Crash landings are all part of the fun, but this crash wasn't an accident.

I JUST LOST CONTROL OF IT. I DON'T KNOW WHAT HAPPENED.

HERE'S YOUR ANSWER, ALEX. A COUPLE OF PIECES OF CHEWED-UP GUM —WILDBERRY BUBBLE GUM, TO BE EXACT.

SOMEONE SABOTAGED YOUR PLANE, ALEX.

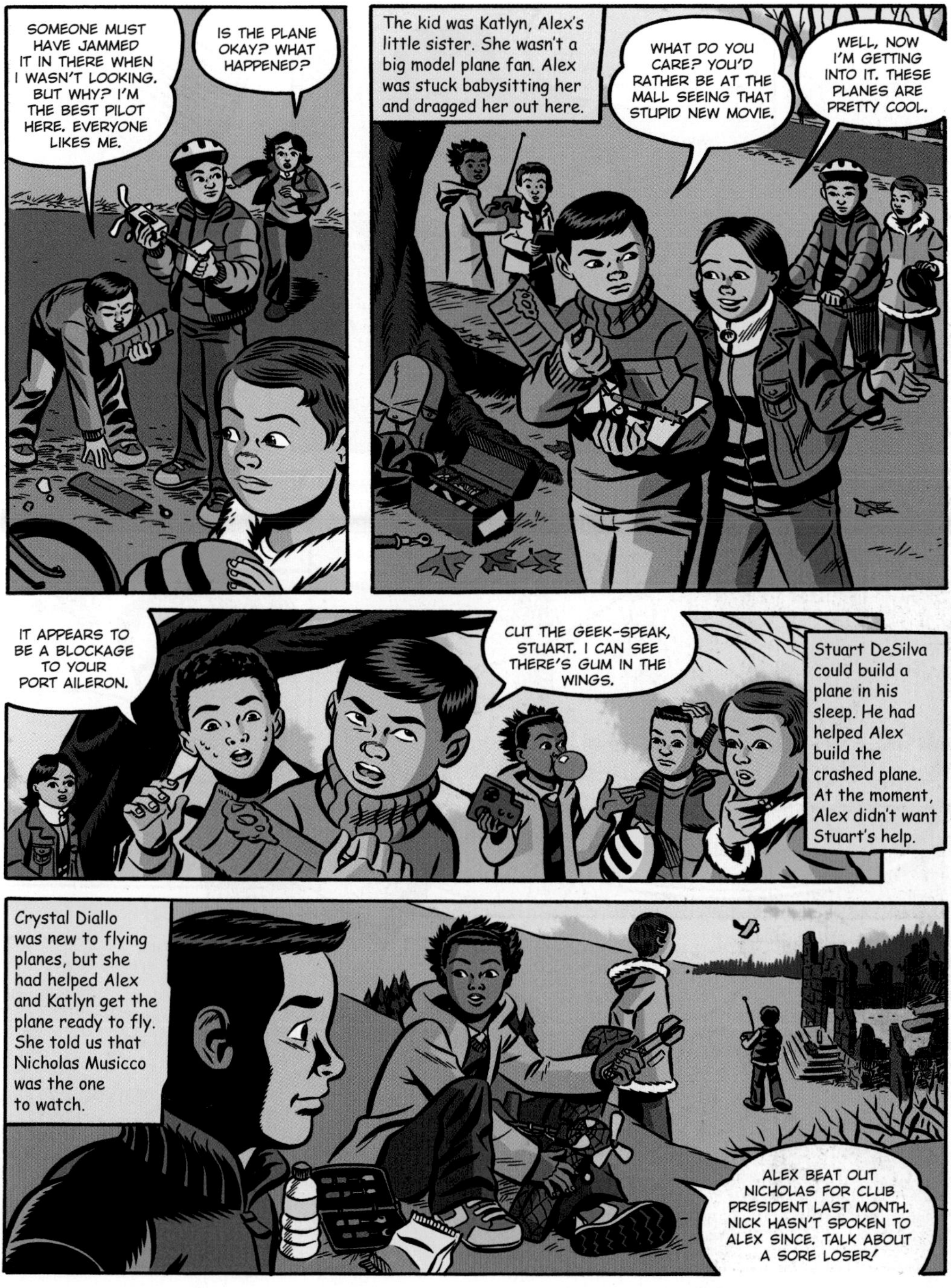
SOMEONE MUST HAVE JAMMED IT IN THERE WHEN I WASN'T LOOKING. BUT WHY? I'M THE BEST PILOT HERE. EVERYONE LIKES ME.
IS THE PLANE OKAY? WHAT HAPPENED?
The kid was Katlyn, Alex's little sister. She wasn't a big model plane fan. Alex was stuck babysitting her and dragged her out here.
WHAT DO YOU CARE? YOU'D RATHER BE AT THE MALL SEEING THAT STUPID NEW MOVIE.
WELL, NOW I'M GETTING INTO IT. THESE PLANES ARE PRETTY COOL.
IT APPEARS TO BE A BLOCKAGE TO YOUR PORT AILERON.
CUT THE GEEK-SPEAK, STUART. I CAN SEE THERE'S GUM IN THE WINGS.
Stuart DeSilva could build a plane in his sleep. He had helped Alex build the crashed plane. At the moment, Alex didn't want Stuart's help.
Crystal Diallo was new to flying planes, but she had helped Alex and Katlyn get the plane ready to fly. She told us that Nicholas Musicco was the one to watch.
ALEX BEAT OUT NICHOLAS FOR CLUB PRESIDENT LAST MONTH. NICK HASN'T SPOKEN TO ALEX SINCE. TALK ABOUT A SORE LOSER!

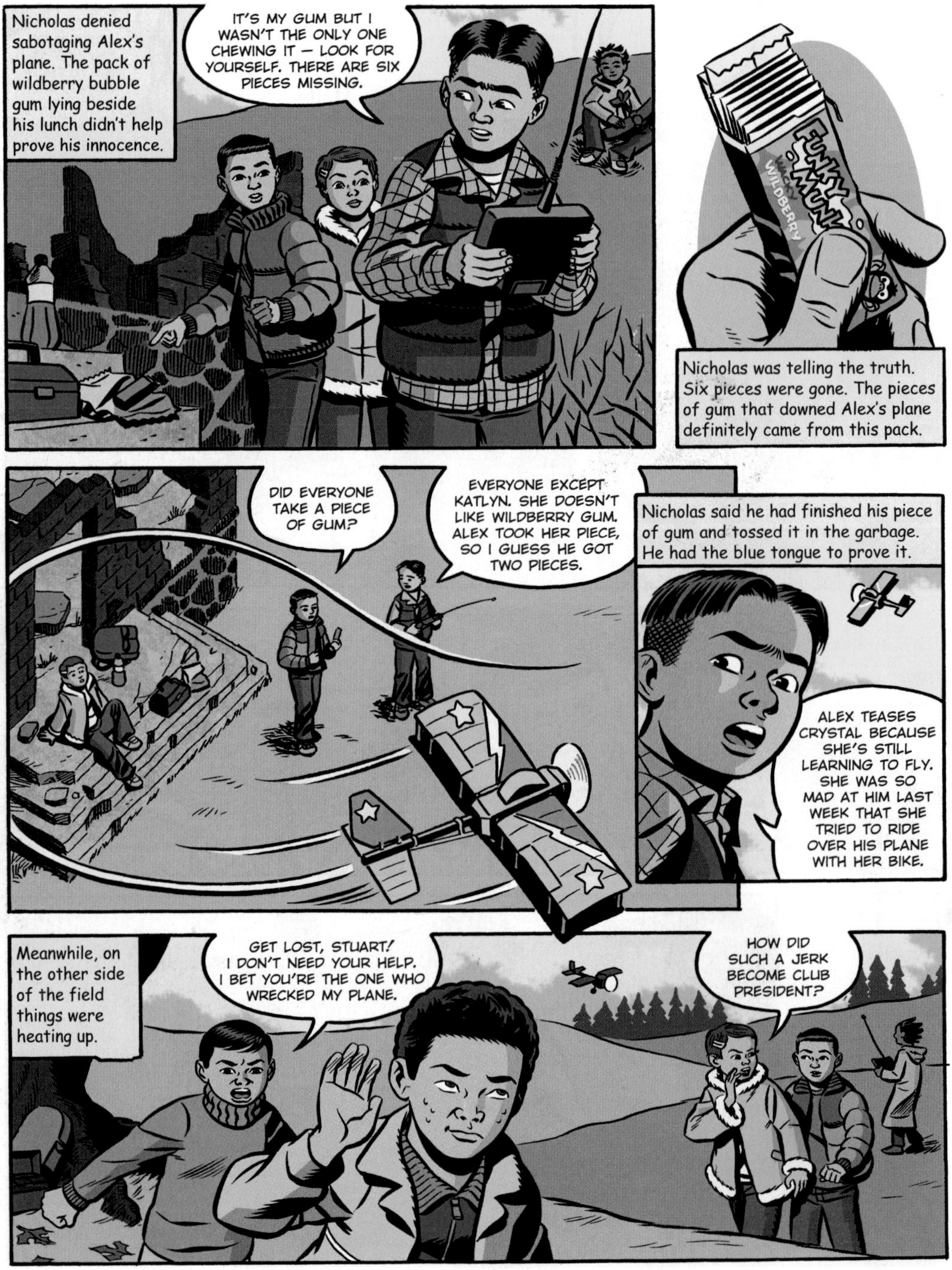
Nicholas denied sabotaging Alex's plane. The pack of wildberry bubble gum lying beside his lunch didn't help prove his innocence.
IT'S MY GUM BUT I WASN'T THE ONLY ONE CHEWING IT — LOOK FOR YOURSELF. THERE ARE SIX PIECES MISSING.
WILDBERRY
Nicholas was telling the truth. Six pieces were gone. The pieces of gum that downed Alex's plane definitely came from this pack.
DID EVERYONE TAKE A PIECE OF GUM?
EVERYONE EXCEPT KATLYN. SHE DOESN'T LIKE WILDBERRY GUM. ALEX TOOK HER PIECE, SO I GUESS HE GOT TWO PIECES.
Nicholas said he had finished his piece of gum and tossed it in the garbage. He had the blue tongue to prove it.
ALEX TEASES CRYSTAL BECAUSE SHE'S STILL LEARNING TO FLY. SHE WAS SO MAD AT HIM LAST WEEK THAT SHE TRIED TO RIDE OVER HIS PLANE WITH HER BIKE.
Meanwhile, on the other side of the field things were heating up.
GET LOST, STUART! I DON'T NEED YOUR HELP. I BET YOU'RE THE ONE WHO WRECKED MY PLANE.
HOW DID SUCH A JERK BECOME CLUB PRESIDENT?

Stuart and Alex had built the plane together, but Stuart had done all the hard work.

THAT LOUDMOUTH DOESN'T KNOW A WING TIP FROM A COCKPIT. NOW HE'LL HAVE TO TAKE KATLYN TO SEE THAT SAPPY MOVIE AT THE MALL.

On the way home from the field, things didn't get better for Alex.

WHERE ARE THOSE PIECES OF GUM? I KNOW I PUT THEM IN THIS POCKET!

WILDBERRY GUM. YECH!

THERE GOES NICHOLAS. I DON'T THINK HE'S TELLING US THE WHOLE STORY.

LET'S TAIL HIM AND FIND OUT.

Rodriguez

We followed Nicholas for almost an hour. He grabbed some lunch and then headed to the mall. We were ready to give up our surveillance when things got interesting.

NOW PLAYING 1 The PRINCESS DIAPERS 2

PRINCESS DIAPERS 2

the Hobby Hut

YOU SHOULD HAVE BEEN THERE, DONALD! THE GUM TOTALLY MESSED UP ALEX'S PLANE. IT WAS SO FUNNY!

MODEL TRAINS 30% OFF

LOWER THE LANDING GEAR, MAX. I KNOW WHO CRASHED THE PLANE.

Do you know who crashed Alex's plane? All the clues are here. Turn to page 74 for the solution.

Morse Message

Alex sent Max and Alison a note. The problem is he wrote it in Morse code. **What does the note say?**

--/.-/-.../...//-.-/-.-/.../-.../.-/-../.-/...//---/-.

--/.-/-.../...//-.-/-.-/.../-.../.-/-../.-/...//---/-.

-/...-/.-/-.../-.-/...//---/-.//...-/---/.-../.-/..../..-/.-/--.//

-/....../..-/-.../..-/...//---/-.//---/.-/.-//...../.../-../..-/.-/--.//

-/....././//--/-.-/....-/-/-.-/-.-/.-//---/---/..-/---/---//

-.../.-/...-/....-/...-/.//-.../---/.-/-.-/.-/.-/.-//--.-/---/---//

-..././/./-..././//--.-/.-.-/..././/.../..../...--/.././/-//

-..././-.././/.-/---/-.-/.-../..../.-/../.-./...//.-/...-///

-.././../-.././-.-/--//.../...-/.-/---/-.././//./.-///

-.-/---/---/..././/-..././///.-/-/.-/.-/-.-/-.././/---/---///

TIP: Morse code is written with a slash (/) between letters and a double slash (//) between words.

Morse code symbols:

A .-	J .---	S ...
B -...	K -.-	T -
C -.-.	L .-..	U ..-
D -..	M --	V ...-
E .	N -.	W .--
F ..-.	O ---	X -..-
G --.	P .--.	Y -.--
H	Q --.-	Z --..
I ..	R .-.	

ANSWER PAGE 82

The Case of the...

Lucky Skates

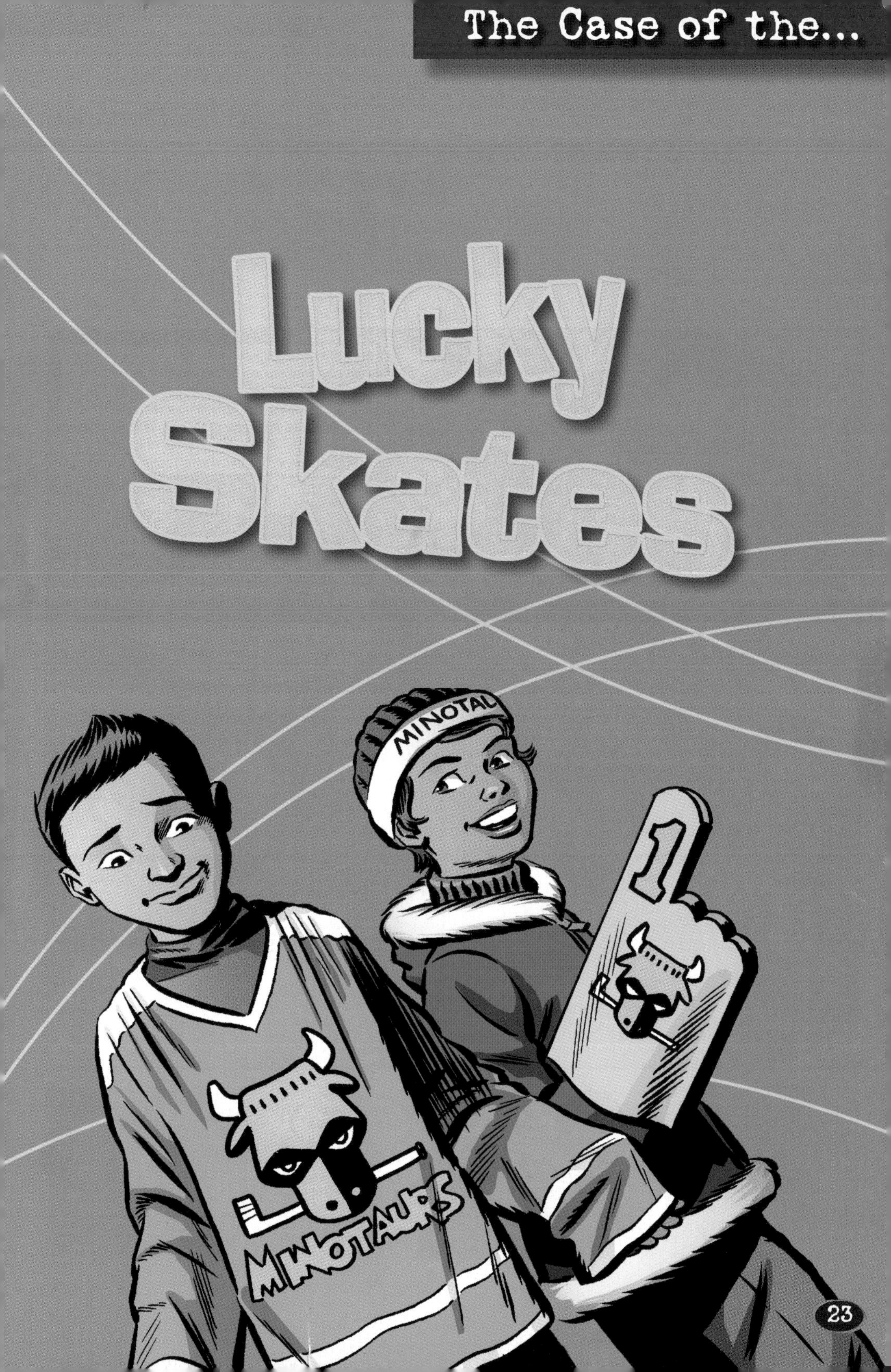
MINOTAU
1
MINOTAURS

The Case of the Lucky Skates

Did you know hockey pucks are frozen so they won't bounce during games? Max Finder here, Grade 7 detective and reluctant hockey fan. It's just before the playoff game between the Meadows Minotaurs and the Timber Creek Titans. Alison dragged me along to cheer for the Minotaurs, her brother's team.

I KNOW YOU'D RATHER BE READING A DETECTIVE BOOK, MAX, BUT TRY TO LOOK EXCITED. ROLL UP YOUR SLEEVES AND NO ONE WILL KNOW YOU'RE WEARING MY DAD'S SHIRT.

We were on our way to the stands when Tony DeMatteo, the star of the Minotaurs, came running from the dressing room.

MAX, ALISON, SOMEBODY SNAGGED MY SKATES!

Tony is set to beat the record for the most goals scored in a season. A few months ago, Dimitri Kozlov, the NHL hockey star, signed Tony's skates.

THEY'RE OLD SKATES, BUT SINCE THE RUSSIAN ROCKET SIGNED THEM, I'VE BEEN A SCORING MACHINE! I'LL NEED THEM IF I'M GOING TO BEAT THAT RECORD AND WIN THE PLAYOFF GAME.

Tony often forgets that hockey is a team sport. His ego is the size of an NHL player's paycheque. But the guy looked desperate, and so did Alison. I guess the thought of Tony missing out on the playoff game was too much for her.

WE'LL FIND THOSE SKATES, TONY.

START FROM THE BEGINNING AND TELL US WHAT HAPPENED.

I arrived early to grab lunch before the game. I sat with right winger Lorrisa Swart. Her whole family plays hockey. Basher McGintley was there too. Basher plays defence, but I think he wishes he could score more goals.

I'M GOING TO THE WASHROOM. CAN YOU WATCH MY BAG, LORRISA?

SURE THING, TONY.

Lorrisa didn't do a good job of watching my bag. When I got back she was gone. So was Basher. The two Titans players were still there and they were up to something.

HEY THERE, MIGHTY MINOTAUR!

HOPE YOUR SKATES ARE EXTRA LUCKY TODAY. YOU'RE GOING TO NEED THEM!

I like to settle scores on the ice, so I ignored the Titan losers and dropped off my bag in the dressing room. I didn't have time to see if those goons took my skates, because Coach Coleman wanted the team out in the stands to go over our strategy.

REMEMBER TO WORK THE ZONE DEFENCE, PASS THE PUCK, AND KEEP YOUR HEADS UP.

BACK IN THE DRESSING ROOM, I CHECKED MY BAG AND MY SKATES WERE GONE!

SOMEBODY DOESN'T WANT YOU PLAYING IN THIS GAME...

...OR THE MINOTAURS WINNING THE FINALS.

Tony went back to the dressing room, and Alison and I went back to the snack bar. Doug Chang was cleaning up after the pre-game rush. I asked if he'd seen anything strange.

LORRISA KNOCKED OVER THAT GARBAGE CAN WITH HER BLUE HOCKEY BAG. THAT THING WAS SO BIG SHE COULDN'T CARRY IT! SHE JUST DRAGGED IT ACROSS THE FLOOR.

On the floor near the girls' washroom, we turned up an important clue.

IT'S A BLADE GUARD FROM A HOCKEY SKATE.

Tony D.

It was pretty easy to see who the guard belonged to. I checked out the garbage, but it was empty. The bag had been changed.

I talked to the arena caretaker while Alison checked out the girls' washroom. She ran into Nanda Kanwar, who plays goalie and was all geared up for the game.

I HEAR SIMON SWART ISN'T HAPPY ABOUT TONY TRYING TO BREAK HIS HIGH-SCORE RECORD. SIMON HAS HELD THAT RECORD FOR FIVE YEARS AND WANTS TO PLAY IN THE NHL.

I found the caretaker, Gary, behind the hockey rink. Gary drives the Zamboni that cleans the ice. He didn't see any skates in the garbage.

BUT I DID SEE A SHORT GUY WITH GLASSES SNOOPING AROUND THE MINOTAURS' DRESSING ROOM WHILE THE WHOLE TEAM WAS SITTING IN THE STANDS. HE WAS WEARING A TITANS JACKET, SO I TOLD HIM TO GET LOST.

Alison stuck her head out of the girls' washroom window. She was worried. The start of the game was only a few minutes away and the skates were still missing. I wanted to find Gary's dressing room snoop.

NO SKATES IN HERE, MAX. ANY OTHER IDEAS?

CHECK OUT THE MINOTAURS' DRESSING ROOM. I'M HEADING INTO TITAN TERRITORY.

Sitting behind the Titans' bench wasn't the smartest idea I've had in my detective career, but it did get me close to the dressing room snoop. He was talking to the Titans' coach.

GO TITANS

ANY LUCK IN THE DRESSING ROOM, RON?

Before I could hear the snoop's answer, the Titans came out from their dressing room and sat on the bench.

HEY THERE, LITTLE MINOTAUR. I THINK YOU'RE IN THE WRONG SECTION.

While I was fleeing the Titans' turf, Alison was checking out the Minotaurs' dressing room.

WHERE ARE THEY, LORRISA?

KEEP LOOKING, BASHER. I KNOW I PUT THEM IN MY HOCKEY BAG.

THE GAME STARTS IN A FEW MINUTES AND I STILL DON'T HAVE MY LUCKY SKATES.

DON'T WORRY. WE'LL GET YOU ON THE ICE.

GET READY FOR THE FACEOFF, TONY! I KNOW WHO TOOK YOUR SKATES AND WHERE THEY'RE HIDDEN.

Do you know who took Tony's lucky skates? All the clues are here. Turn to page 75 to find out.

27

Coach's Corner

Coach Coleman is filling in the Meadows Minotaurs' scoring chart. **Use the clues to find out who is the leading scorer on the team.**

Meadows Minotaurs

Player	Number	Position	Goals	Assists	Penalty Minutes
Tony DeMatteo	17	Left Wing	--	13	3
Basher McGintley	6	Defence	3	9	7
Lorrisa Swart	12	Right Wing	--	14	1
Marcus Santos	8	Left Wing	9	19	3
Alex Rodriguez	21	Defence	--	22	2
Leslie Chang	3	Centre	--	19	1
Josh Spodek	18	Defence	--	16	5
Layne Jennings	15	Defence	10	18	2
Nicholas Musicco	7	Right Wing	--	24	4
Nanda Kanwar	31	Goalie	0	3	0

Clues:

- Leslie has scored twice as many goals as Lorrisa.
- Lorrisa has scored in just two games, but got a hat trick (three goals) each time.
- Nicholas has five more goals than Layne, but two fewer than Alex.
- Josh has scored half as many goals as Leslie.
- Tony has scored twice as many goals as Alex.

ANSWER PAGE 82

ANGRY ANCHORMAN

The Case of the ANGRY ANCHORMAN

Did you know the world's hairiest donkey is the *Poitou* from France? Max Finder here, fact collector and Grade 7 detective. My class is at our local TV station to present the money we raised for their children's charity. That woman talking to us works at the station. She is also my mom.

WELCOME TO CKWM, EVERYONE! AND A VERY SPECIAL WELCOME TO MY SON. I'LL TRY NOT TO EMBARRASS YOU, MAX.

TOO LATE FOR THAT!

GREEN ROOM

7 C

Jan 09/07
CKWM Children's Fund $510⁰⁰
Five hundred and ten———⁰⁰/₁₀₀

ARRGH!

OUCH!

The guy covered in plant dirt is Bull O'Wiley, CKWM's news anchor and big boss at the station. The kid is Kyle Kressman. He loves practical jokes, but this one had accident written all over it.

WATCH WHERE YOU'RE STANDING, YOU LITTLE TWERP!

THAT'S ENOUGH, KYLE!

A few seconds later, I wasn't the only one in an embarrassing situation.

WATCH WHERE YOU'RE WALKING!

Our teacher, Mr. Reed, chewed Kyle out for tripping Bull. Kyle sulked off to the bathroom and stayed there.

GREEN ROOM

WHERE HAVE YOU BEEN, URSULA? HAVE YOU SEEN KYLE?

WHAT? NO. I WAS TALKING TO DEB, THE MAKEUP ARTIST.

Ursula's father also worked at the station, so she knew a lot of the adults here. The waiting around was making us thirsty, so we joined her at the snack table.

I SPILLED SOME JUICE. THE TABLE COULD BE STICKY.

DOESN'T FEEL STICKY TO ME.

THAT'S BECAUSE SHE USED HALF A FOREST'S WORTH OF NAPKINS.

MAX, ALISON, WE HAVE A PROBLEM.

We followed Mom to Bull O'Wiley's dressing room. He was there, but his hair wasn't.

SOMEONE STOLE MR. O'WILEY'S WIG, ER, HIS HAIR.

SOMEONE? IT WASN'T SOMEONE. IT WAS ONE OF THOSE KIDS! I CAN'T GO ON TV LOOKING LIKE A BOILED EGG.

It was my mom's bright idea to bring us to the station, but now it looked like it was backfiring.

LISTEN KID, FIND MY HAIR BEFORE FIVE O'CLOCK OR YOUR MOM WILL BE WORKING ON THE LATE NEWS UNTIL YOU GRADUATE!

Mr. O'Wiley was in the makeup room when his wig was stolen. Deb was putting on Bull's camera makeup when the wig disappeared, but she didn't see anything.

BULL ALWAYS TAKES OFF HIS WIG WHEN I DO HIS MAKEUP. I PUT IT ON THE WIG STAND BEHIND ME. WHEN I TURNED AROUND, IT WAS GONE.

URSULA WAS HERE FOR A WHILE. THEN SHE WENT TO GET ME A COFFEE. FRAN, THE WEATHERPERSON, DROPPED BY.

With Bull's hair gone, Deb said that Fran would probably read tonight's news. Fran had always wanted to read the news, but Bull made sure she never got a chance.

We bumped into Ursula on our way to see Fran. She said she saw the wig on its stand when she left Deb. Last year, Deb worked with Ursula's dad. But Bull got mad at him and he's been stuck working on the late news ever since.

MY DAD LEAVES FOR WORK JUST AS I GET HOME FROM SCHOOL. I ONLY SEE HIM ON WEEKENDS.

Fran said the wig wasn't on the stand when she dropped by the makeup room. She also remembered passing Ursula in the hallway.

I REMEMBER SEEING URSULA. SHE LOOKED SO HOT IN THAT HEAVY JACKET. OH YEAH, I CAUGHT THAT KYLE KID SNOOPING AROUND, TOO. YOU BETTER FIND HIM BEFORE THE SECURITY GUARDS DO.

STUDIO 1

HEY, KID. GET OUT OF THERE!

KYLE!

THERE HE IS!

THERE YOU ARE! YOU'RE SUPPOSED TO STAY IN THE GREEN ROOM!

WHAT WERE YOU DOING IN THERE, KYLE?

PAYBACK FOR BULL O'WILEY. NOBODY GETS ME IN TROUBLE AND GETS AWAY WITH IT. WANT GUM?

THE NEWS STARTS IN FIVE MINUTES, LITTLE DETECTIVES. WHERE'S MY HAIR?

START PRACTISING YOUR LINES, MR. O'WILEY. I KNOW WHERE YOUR WIG IS.

AND THE THIEF IS IN THIS ROOM.

Do you know who hijacked Bull O'Wiley's hair and where it's hidden? All the clues are here. Turn to page 76 for the answer.

NEWSCAST MAD LIB

What's in the news? Ask a friend to complete the blanks in these news stories. Then read it aloud together.

Welcome to tonight's newscast.
I'm [your name]. In our top story, the city of [type of cheese] was in chaos today after a [wild animal] jumped out of a [large appliance] and ran up and down the street in a [article of clothing]. Traffic came to a standstill, and a passerby cried out for [name of super-hero]. The police asked [famous singer] to sing [kids' song] to calm everybody down. Then they instructed the crowds to head for [far-off country]. The city is finally as quiet as a [musical instrument] this evening.

Now for sports: the [dog treat] beat the [type of fish] today thanks to the efforts of [a friend's mom]. And the [exotic animal] outscored the [fruit] in overtime. [Name of family pet] has decided to retire from [extreme sport] to take up [kind of dance]. Finally, [famous basketball star] will be travelling to [your school] tomorrow night to teach kids all about [favourite video game] and [type of junk food].

And in weather, for the first time in [big number] years, [vegetable] fell from the sky during a freak storm. Luckily, [television character] gathered it up and made [your favourite meal] out of it. For tomorrow, it looks like it'll be raining cats and [type of bug]. So, be sure to carry a [school supply] with you. That's tonight's news. Good night, and remember to keep your [body part] in your pocket.

The Case of the...

Missing Manga

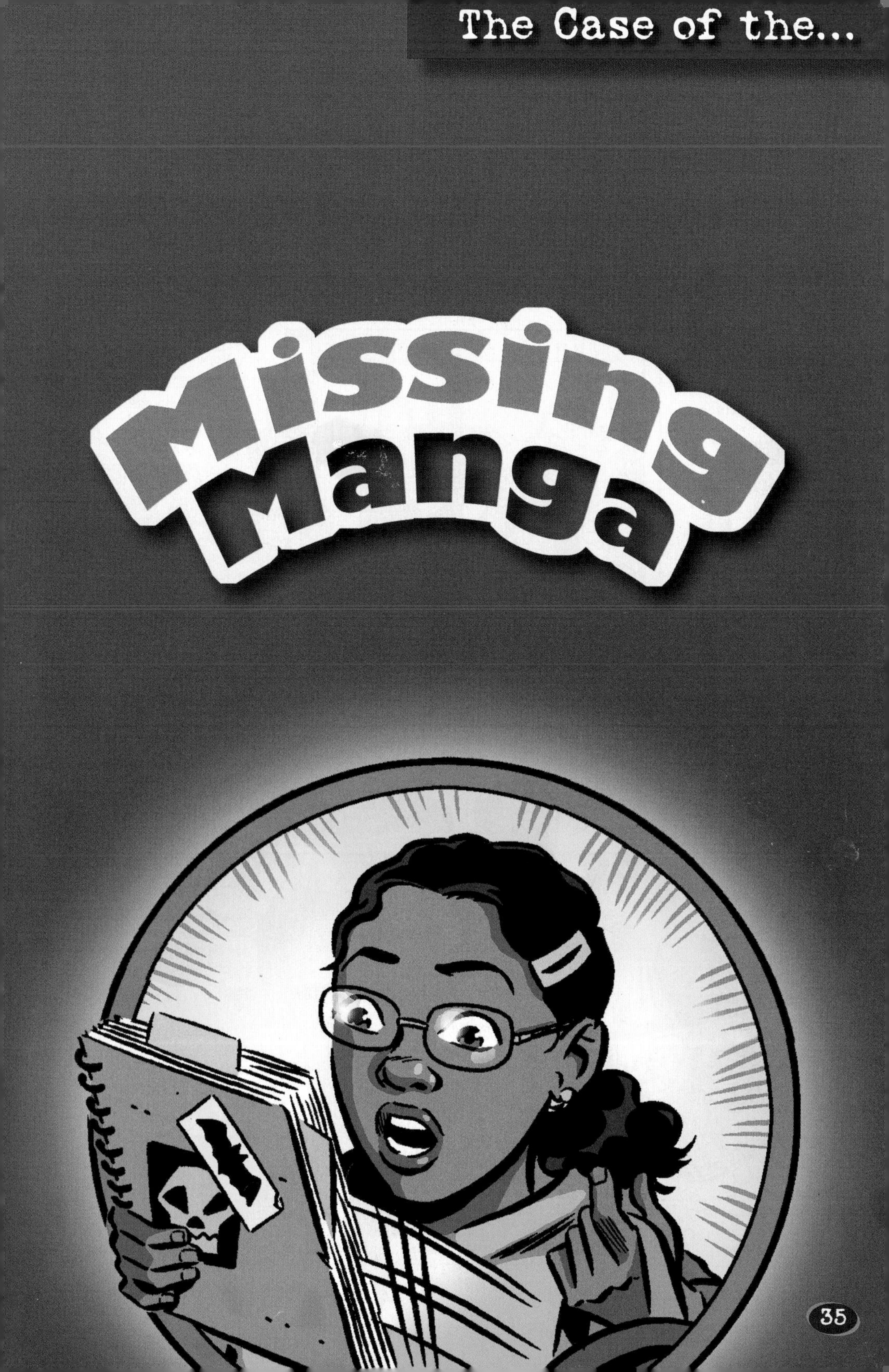

The Case of the Missing Manga

Max Finder here, fact collector, Grade 7 detective, and very late manga fan.

Kengo Takahashi, one of my favourite artists, is launching his new manga series at the comic shop.

MAX! YOU'RE AN HOUR LATE. WHERE HAVE YOU BEEN?

I GOT SUCKED INTO THE FINAL LEVEL OF *PATCHET AND CLUNK* AND LOST TRACK OF TIME.

DID I MISS MUCH?

JUST EVERYTHING.

LUCKY FOR YOU I TOOK SOME PICS.

Our friend, Sarah Khadda, won an autographed page from Takahashi's new series.

Sarah introduced her comic-loving friend, Crystal Diallo, to Takahashi.

While Crystal was getting a headband for her hair, Sarah got drawing tips.

Alison snapped one last photo of Crystal and Sarah with Takahashi.

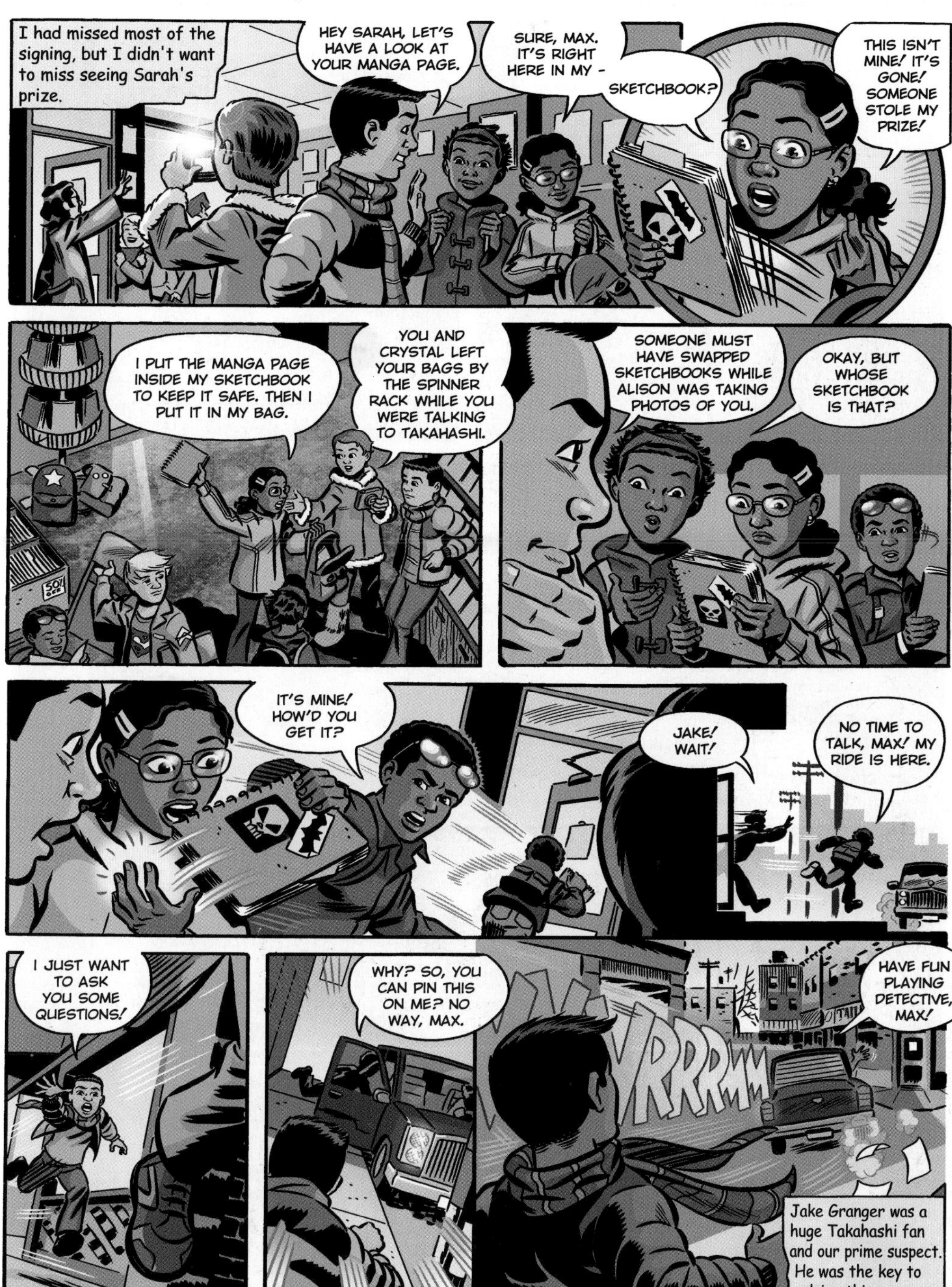
I had missed most of the signing, but I didn't want to miss seeing Sarah's prize.
HEY SARAH, LET'S HAVE A LOOK AT YOUR MANGA PAGE.
SURE, MAX. IT'S RIGHT HERE IN MY -
SKETCHBOOK?
THIS ISN'T MINE! IT'S GONE! SOMEONE STOLE MY PRIZE!
I PUT THE MANGA PAGE INSIDE MY SKETCHBOOK TO KEEP IT SAFE. THEN I PUT IT IN MY BAG.
YOU AND CRYSTAL LEFT YOUR BAGS BY THE SPINNER RACK WHILE YOU WERE TALKING TO TAKAHASHI.
SOMEONE MUST HAVE SWAPPED SKETCHBOOKS WHILE ALISON WAS TAKING PHOTOS OF YOU.
OKAY, BUT WHOSE SKETCHBOOK IS THAT?
IT'S MINE! HOW'D YOU GET IT?
JAKE! WAIT!
NO TIME TO TALK, MAX! MY RIDE IS HERE.
I JUST WANT TO ASK YOU SOME QUESTIONS!
WHY? SO, YOU CAN PIN THIS ON ME? NO WAY, MAX.
VRRRMM
HAVE FUN PLAYING DETECTIVE, MAX!
Jake Granger was a huge Takahashi fan and our prime suspect. He was the key to solving this case.

Meanwhile, Alison wasn't having much luck with Travis, the comic shop clerk.

ALL I SAW WAS A BUNCH OF KIDS THUMBING THROUGH COMICS.

I DON'T TRUST TRAVIS. HE WAS HANGING AROUND THE SPINNER RACK. AND HE SELLS ANIME STUFF ON THE WEB.

I BET HE COULD GET A GOOD PRICE FOR YOUR MANGA PAGE.

We caught a bus home and that gave us a chance to talk to Crystal.

DID YOU SEE ANYONE NEAR SARAH'S BAG?

NO. I WAS GETTING MY PHOTOS TAKEN WITH SARAH AND TAKAHASHI THE WHOLE TIME.

DINGG!

WE WERE GOING TO WORK ON OUR COMIC THIS AFTERNOON.

I SAW HER MOM EARLIER. SHE'S OFF WORK TODAY.

THIS IS MY STOP. I'LL SEE YOU TOMORROW SARAH.

WE CAN DO THAT AT SCHOOL. I'VE GOT TO BABYSIT MY BROTHER UNTIL MY MOM GETS BACK FROM WORK.

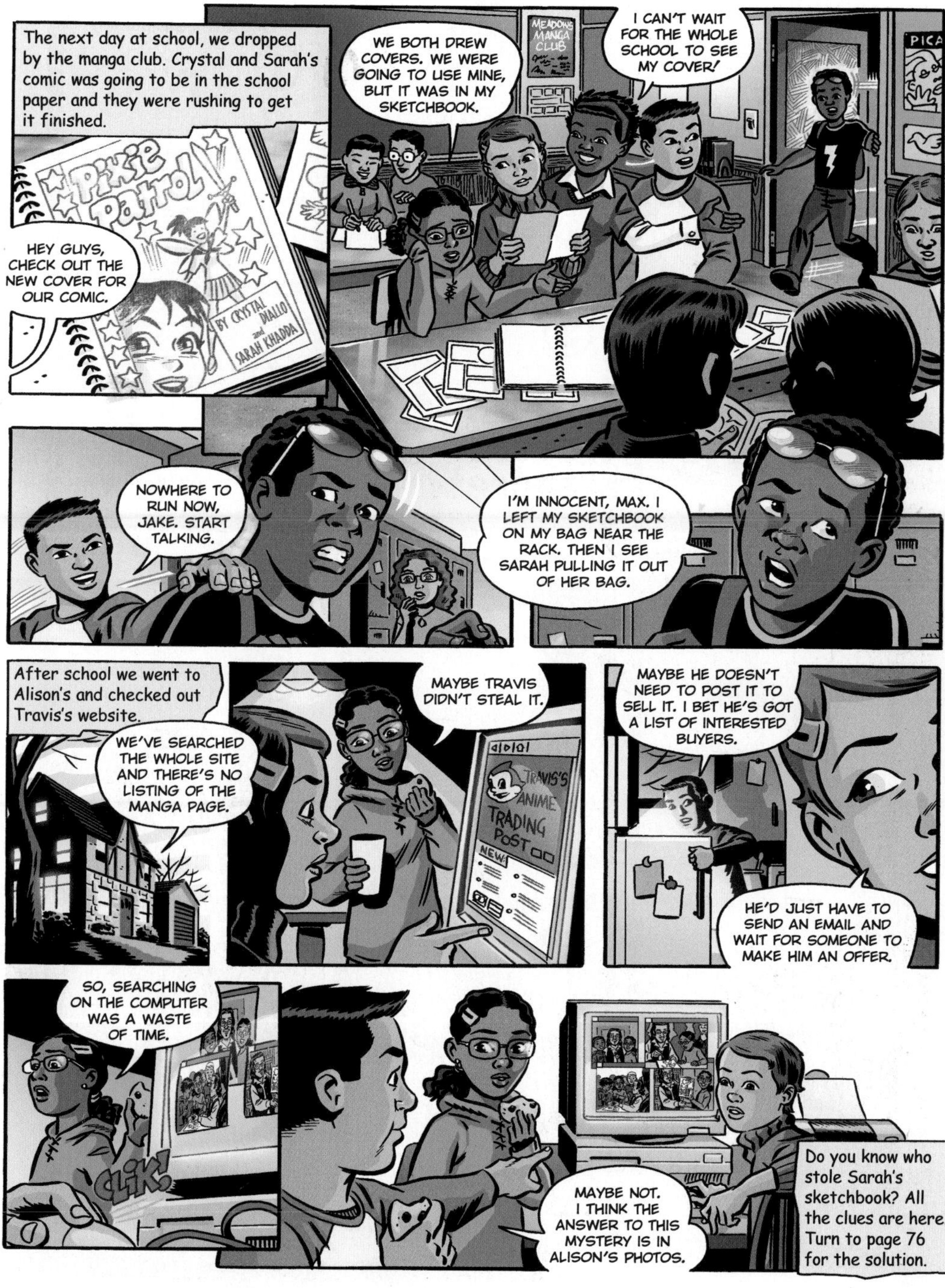

The next day at school, we dropped by the manga club. Crystal and Sarah's comic was going to be in the school paper and they were rushing to get it finished.
Pixie Patrol
BY CRYSTAL DIALLO and SARAH KHADDA
HEY GUYS, CHECK OUT THE NEW COVER FOR OUR COMIC.
WE BOTH DREW COVERS. WE WERE GOING TO USE MINE, BUT IT WAS IN MY SKETCHBOOK.
MEADOWS MANGA CLUB
I CAN'T WAIT FOR THE WHOLE SCHOOL TO SEE MY COVER!
NOWHERE TO RUN NOW, JAKE. START TALKING.
I'M INNOCENT, MAX. I LEFT MY SKETCHBOOK ON MY BAG NEAR THE RACK. THEN I SEE SARAH PULLING IT OUT OF HER BAG.
After school we went to Alison's and checked out Travis's website.
WE'VE SEARCHED THE WHOLE SITE AND THERE'S NO LISTING OF THE MANGA PAGE.
MAYBE TRAVIS DIDN'T STEAL IT.
TRAVIS'S ANIME TRADING POST
NEWS
MAYBE HE DOESN'T NEED TO POST IT TO SELL IT. I BET HE'S GOT A LIST OF INTERESTED BUYERS.
HE'D JUST HAVE TO SEND AN EMAIL AND WAIT FOR SOMEONE TO MAKE HIM AN OFFER.
SO, SEARCHING ON THE COMPUTER WAS A WASTE OF TIME.
CLIK!
MAYBE NOT. I THINK THE ANSWER TO THIS MYSTERY IS IN ALISON'S PHOTOS.
Do you know who stole Sarah's sketchbook? All the clues are here. Turn to page 76 for the solution.

Decode It

This page from Sarah's sketchbook is packed full of pictograms.
Can you decipher the meaning of each one?

① r
T world i
p

② wish
star

③ secret
secret
secret

④ h
g o
n r
i s

⑤ moonceon

⑥ yrotcivyrotciv

⑦ HE
NOW RE

⑧ Dutch
Dutch

⑨ shopshopshopshop
u

⑩ 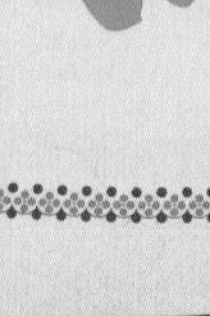 NV

ANSWER PAGE 82

The Case of the...

Elvis Prankster

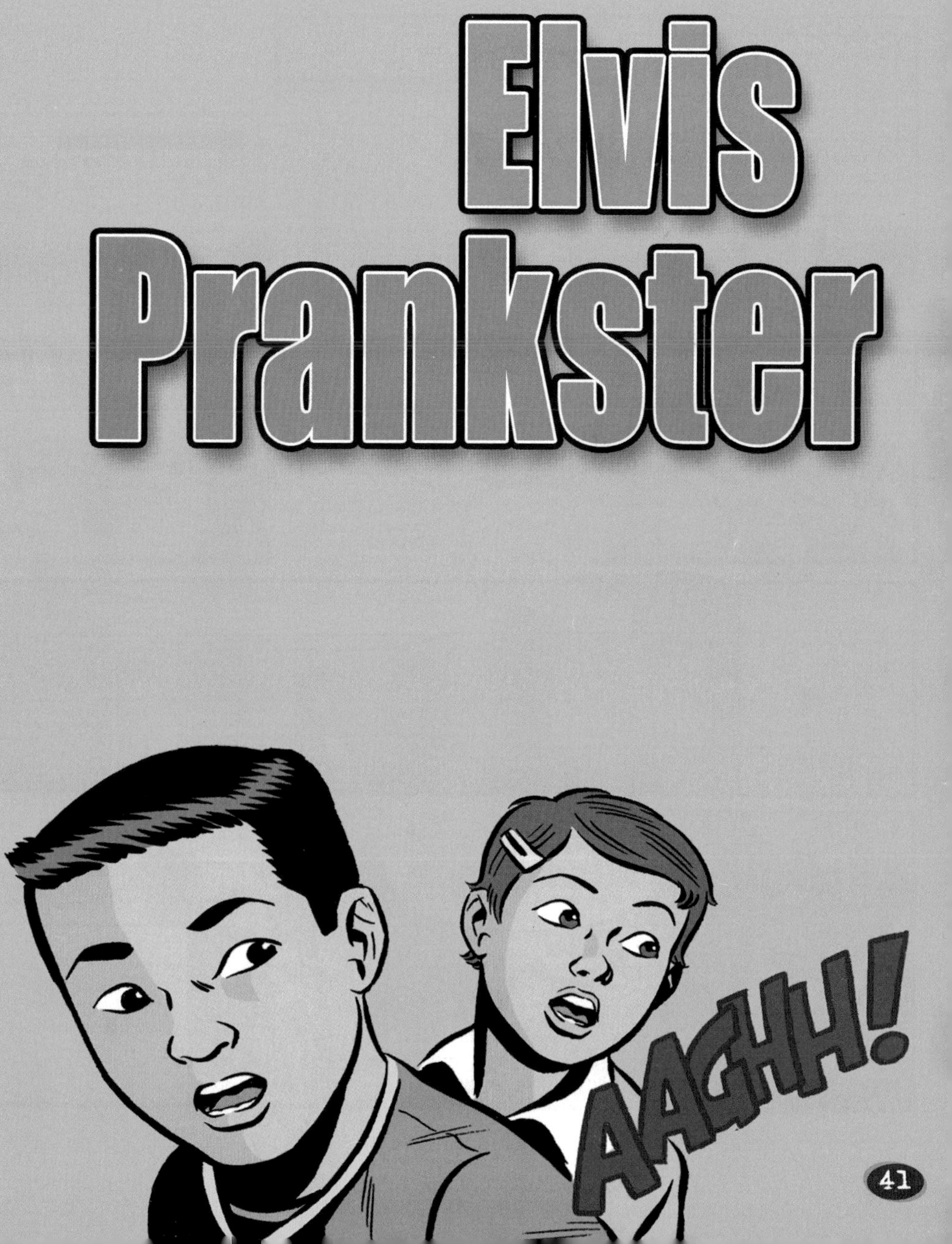
AAGHH!

The Case of the
Elvis Prankster

Did you know that the Basenji breed of dog yodels instead of barks? Max Finder here, fact collector and Grade 7 detective. Alison and I are at the Pilton Meadows Hotel to meet Alison's older brother, Marcus.

LOOKING GOOD, MARCUS! HOW'S THE NEW JOB?

SPECIAL EVENTS
ELVIS CONFERENCE
GRAND BALLROOM
MEADOWS DOG SHOW
JUNIOR BALLROOM

WHAT'S WITH ALL THE DOGS AND ROCK 'N' ROLLERS?

THERE'S A DOG SHOW AND AN ELVIS CONVENTION THIS WEEKEND. IT'S BEEN CRAZY!

Elvis Presley may have been the king of rock 'n' roll, but Nicole Pilton was not a fan. Nicole's father owned the hotel. She was helping organize the dog show.

MARCUS, THESE ELVIS DWEEBS HAVE BEEN UP TO THEIR LAME TRICKS AGAIN!

JUNIOR BALLROOM

MEADOWS DOG SHOW

DEEP-FRIED PEANUT BUTTER SANDWICHES MIGHT HAVE BEEN ELVIS'S FAVOURITE SNACK, BUT THEY ARE NOT FOR DOGS! ONE MORE PRANK AND DADDY WILL KICK EVERY ELVIS OUT OF THIS HOTEL.

NICOLE, WE DIDN'T DO IT!

LOOKS LIKE SOMEONE IS TRYING TO SHUT DOWN THE ELVIS CONVENTION. BUT WHY?

The guys claiming innocence were Alvin Potter and Eric Brady. Eric's competing in the 16-and-under Elvis Impersonator contest. Alvin is the reigning champ, but this year he is 17 and too old to compete.

THE DOG SHOW CONTESTANTS ARE JEALOUS BECAUSE WE GET THE GRAND BALLROOM FOR OUR CONVENTION. THEY'RE STUCK HERE IN THE SMALL BALLROOM.

BUT IF YOU GET KICKED OUT, THEN THEY'LL GET THE GRAND BALLROOM.

MAX, CAN YOU HELP US?

Eric told me that last night someone pulled another prank. Elvis music was blasted through the hotel loudspeakers.

Marcus and Alison went to talk to the hotel chef about the sandwiches. Eric and I questioned the dog show people. Chester Winfield barked out some information.

A THIN ELVIS IN A BLACK LEATHER JACKET CAME IN CARRYING A TRAY OF THOSE VILE SANDWICHES.

YOU WEREN'T EVEN HERE, CHESTER! IT WAS A TALL, THIN ELVIS IN A WHITE CAPE.

The sandwiches came from the hotel. But the chef didn't know who was behind them. The order came over the phone.

WHO DELIVERED THE SANDWICHES TO THE JUNIOR BALLROOM?

NOBODY. THE MAN ON THE PHONE SAID TO LEAVE THEM OUTSIDE ROOM 432. THE MONEY WAS IN AN ENVELOPE BY THE DOOR.

THE SANDWICH BUYER COVERED HIS TRACKS BY PAYING CASH. BUT WE GOT HIS ROOM NUMBER. SO, WHO IS RENTING ROOM 432?

NO ONE. IT'S EMPTY!

The room wasn't rented, so Marcus said it was okay to go in. He gave us the key for room 432. We checked it out.

432

431

DOG SHOW HEADQUARTERS PLEASE KNOCK

MAX, YOU AND ERIC GO IN. I'LL KEEP WATCH OUT HERE.

THE ROOM SHOULD BE EMPTY, BUT THERE'S A VINTAGE ELVIS CAPE COVERED IN RED HAIR. NO TRUE ELVIS FAN WOULD LET IT GET SO DIRTY.

DISH SOAP, PINK FOOD COLOURING, AND MINI-WIGS?

Outside in the hallway, it looked like Nicole and Alvin weren't enemies after all.

432

431

DOG SHOW HEADQUARTERS PLEASE KNOCK

I BET YOU'RE THE ELVIS PRANKSTER. IF TONIGHT'S SHOW GETS CANCELLED YOU'D STILL GET TO BE THE ELVIS CHAMP.

ME?! YOU AND TINKERBELL ARE MAD BECAUSE YOUR DAD GAVE THE ELVISES THE GRAND BALLROOM.

HEY, NICOLE. HAS YOUR DAD KICKED OUT THE ELVISES YET?

GIVE IT A REST, CHESTER. NOW LEAVE ME ALONE. TINKERBELL NEEDS HER BATH BEFORE TONIGHT'S BIG SHOW.

Next door, I could hear running water. But that wasn't what worried me.

CLICK!

SOMEONE'S COMING! HIDE!!

From our hiding spot in the closet, we could see the Elvis prankster getting ready, but I couldn't make out who it was.

44

Alison trailed the Elvis to the elevator. We left our hiding place and caught up.

WHERE DID THAT ELVIS COME FROM? AND WHERE ARE MAX AND ERIC?

THERE ARE DOZENS OF ELVISES DOWN THERE. WE'LL NEVER FIND THE RIGHT ONE.

WHOEVER IS IN THAT COSTUME TOOK THE ELEVATOR DOWN TO THE LOBBY!

An hour later, everyone was ready for the Elvis impersonator competition, but we hadn't found our mystery Elvis.

MR. PILTON WILL CANCEL THE CONTEST AT THE FIRST SIGN OF ANOTHER ELVIS JOKE.

AAGHH!

THE FOUNTAIN!

ONE OF THOSE ELVIS PEOPLE DID IT! I RECOGNIZED THE WHITE CAPE.

THAT'S IT! TONIGHT'S COMPETITION IS CANCELLED. I WANT EVERY ELVIS OUT OF MY HOTEL!

ELVIS GRAND B

MEADO JUNIOR B

DON'T PACK YOUR BAGS YET. I KNOW WHO THE ELVIS PRANKSTER IS.

Do you know who pulled the pranks? All the clues are here. Turn to page 77 to find out.

45

Photo Play

This puzzle is doggone fun! Only three identical dog photos appear in all three boxes. **Can you find them?**

ANSWER PAGE 82

Gander River Grudge

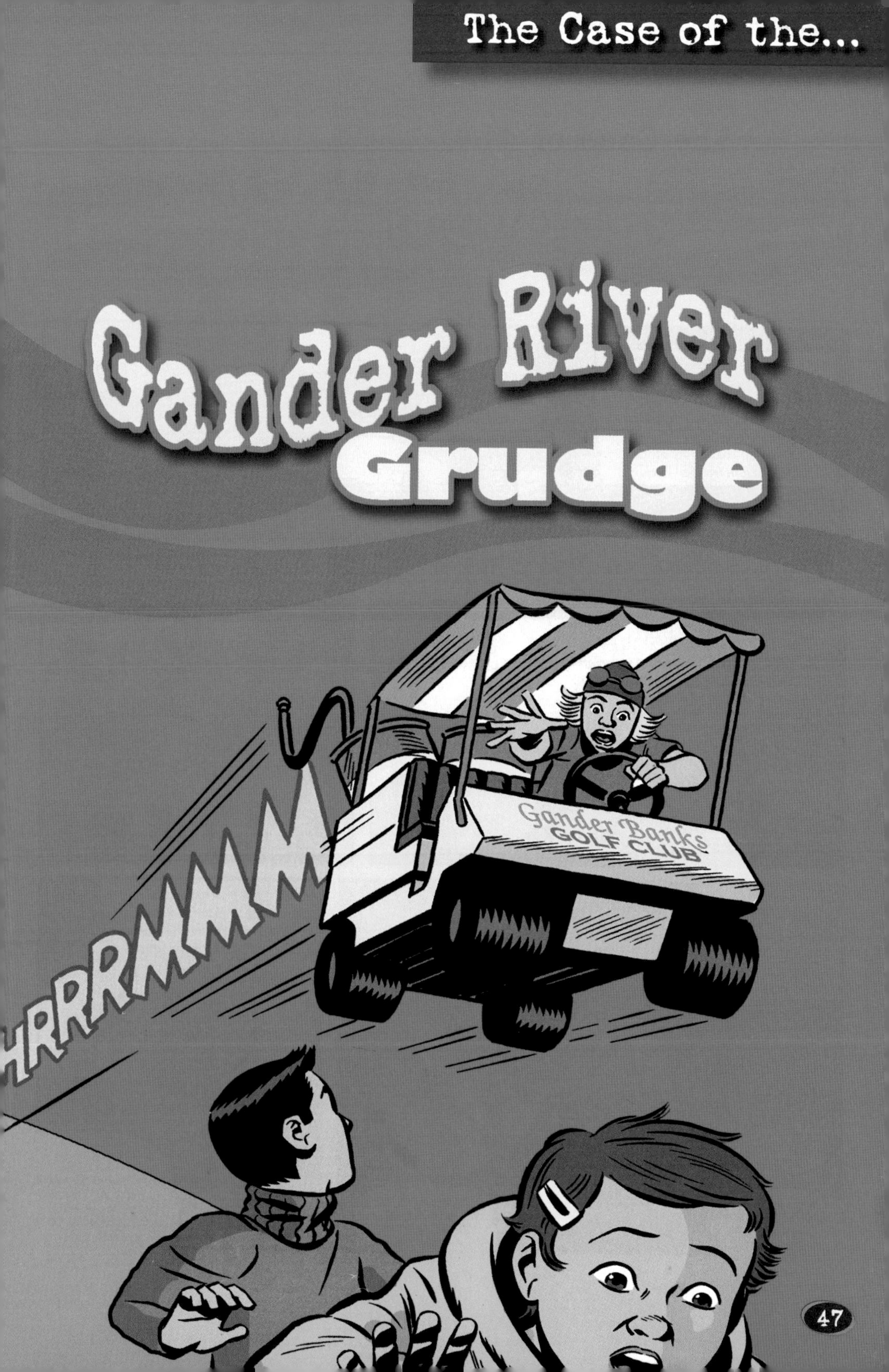
HRRRMMMM
Gander Banks
GOLF CLUB

The Case of the Gander River Grudge

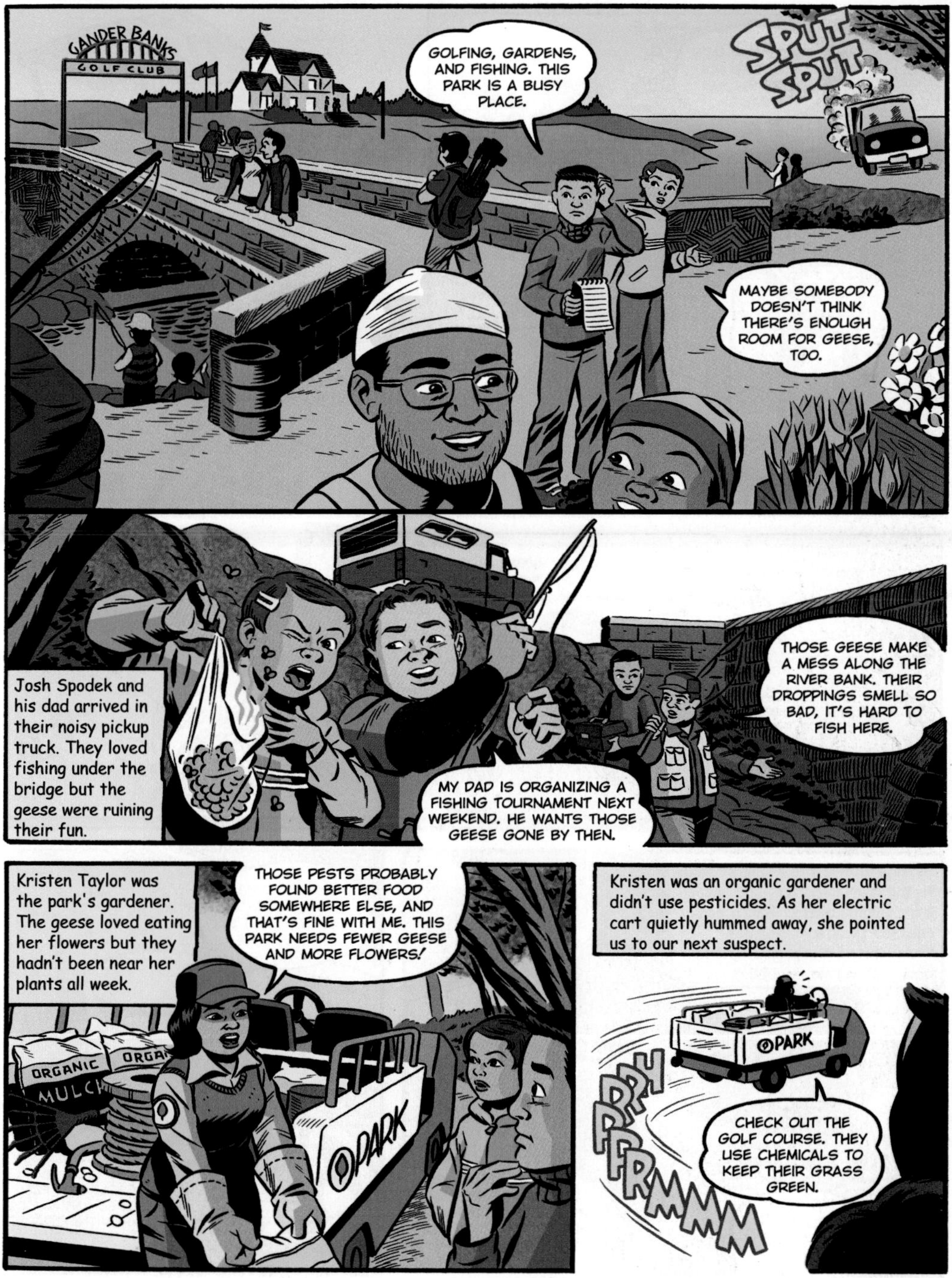
GANDER BANKS
GOLF CLUB
GOLFING, GARDENS, AND FISHING. THIS PARK IS A BUSY PLACE.
SPUT SPUT
MAYBE SOMEBODY DOESN'T THINK THERE'S ENOUGH ROOM FOR GEESE, TOO.
Josh Spodek and his dad arrived in their noisy pickup truck. They loved fishing under the bridge but the geese were ruining their fun.
THOSE GEESE MAKE A MESS ALONG THE RIVER BANK. THEIR DROPPINGS SMELL SO BAD, IT'S HARD TO FISH HERE.
MY DAD IS ORGANIZING A FISHING TOURNAMENT NEXT WEEKEND. HE WANTS THOSE GEESE GONE BY THEN.
Kristen Taylor was the park's gardener. The geese loved eating her flowers but they hadn't been near her plants all week.
THOSE PESTS PROBABLY FOUND BETTER FOOD SOMEWHERE ELSE, AND THAT'S FINE WITH ME. THIS PARK NEEDS FEWER GEESE AND MORE FLOWERS!
ORGANIC MULCH
ORGA
PARK
Kristen was an organic gardener and didn't use pesticides. As her electric cart quietly hummed away, she pointed us to our next suspect.
PARK
RRRH
PPFRMMMM
CHECK OUT THE GOLF COURSE. THEY USE CHEMICALS TO KEEP THEIR GRASS GREEN.

THERE'S PLENTY OF GOOSE POO HERE BUT NO BEANS.

HRRRMMMM

WHAT'S THAT SOUND?

WATCH OUT, LITTLE DUDES!

Zack Eisner was the assistant greenskeeper. He was in charge of keeping the grass green and goose-free.

THOSE LITTLE HONKERS ARE A REAL BUMMER! THEY KEEP COMING BACK TO EAT THE GRASS. I'VE HAD ENOUGH OF THEM.

After we talked to Zack, we went to the animal shelter. The geese were feeling better. Becca had checked the beans out, but hadn't found any poison. They were just normal soybeans.

SOYBEANS CAN MAKE GEESE SICK?

THINGS LIKE SOYBEANS OR BREAD EXPAND INSIDE A GOOSE'S BELLY WHEN THEY EAT THEM. TAKE A LOOK IN THAT JAR, MAX.

THE WET SOYBEAN HAS SOAKED UP THE WATER. IT'S MUCH BIGGER NOW.

NO WONDER THEY WERE SICK. PEOPLE SHOULDN'T FEED GEESE AND DUCKS WHEN THEY GO TO THE PARK.

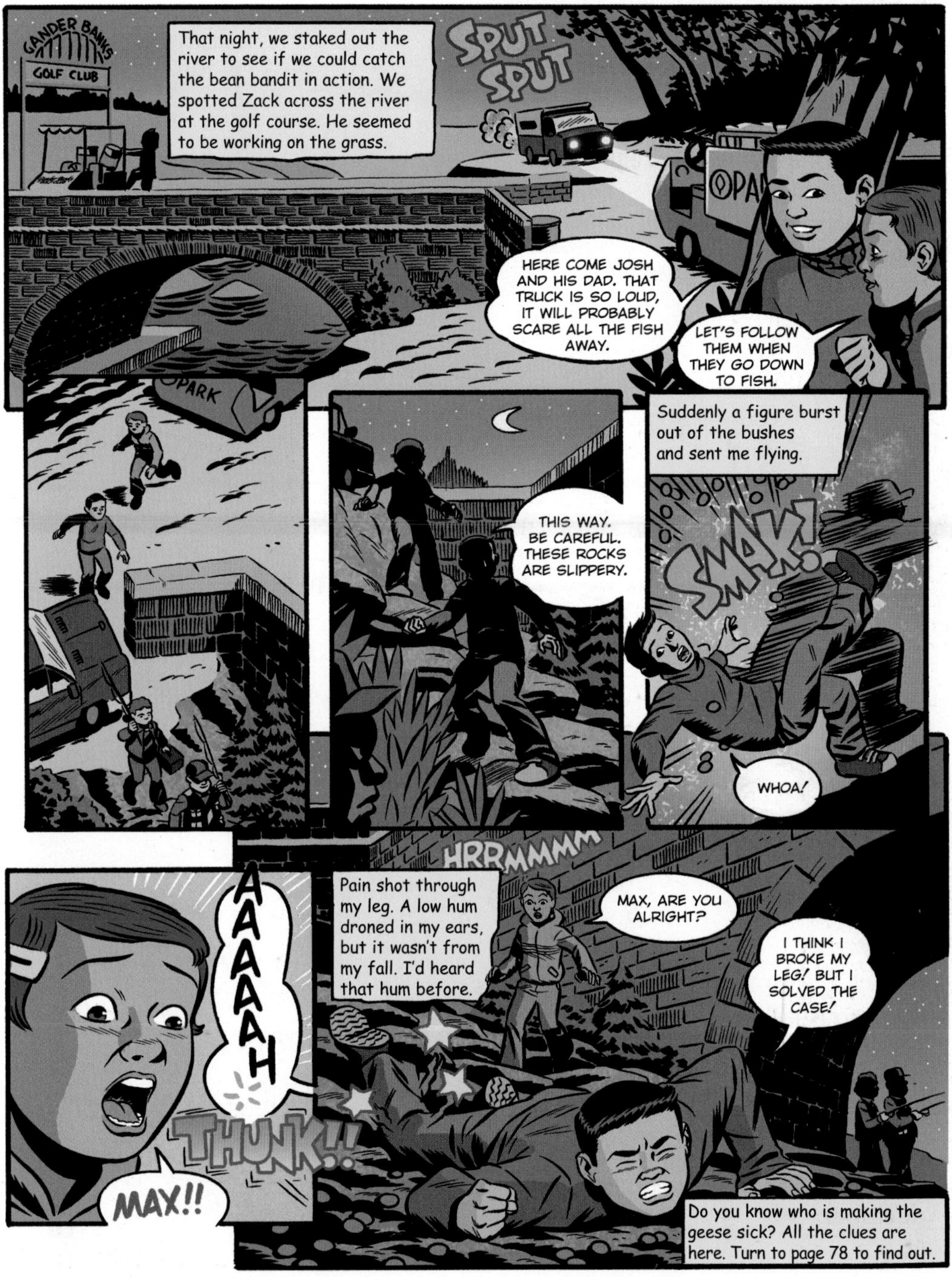
GANDER BANKS
GOLF CLUB
That night, we staked out the river to see if we could catch the bean bandit in action. We spotted Zack across the river at the golf course. He seemed to be working on the grass.
SPUT SPUT
OPARK
HERE COME JOSH AND HIS DAD. THAT TRUCK IS SO LOUD, IT WILL PROBABLY SCARE ALL THE FISH AWAY.
LET'S FOLLOW THEM WHEN THEY GO DOWN TO FISH.
OPARK
THIS WAY. BE CAREFUL. THESE ROCKS ARE SLIPPERY.
Suddenly a figure burst out of the bushes and sent me flying.
SMAK!
WHOA!
HRRMMMM
AAAAAH
THUNK!!
MAX!!
Pain shot through my leg. A low hum droned in my ears, but it wasn't from my fall. I'd heard that hum before.
MAX, ARE YOU ALRIGHT?
I THINK I BROKE MY LEG! BUT I SOLVED THE CASE!
Do you know who is making the geese sick? All the clues are here. Turn to page 78 to find out.

Cast Code

Max helped solve the mystery at Gander River, but he ended up with a broken leg. Alison has signed his cast with this secret message. She's using numbers to represent the letters of the alphabet, so that 1 = A and 26 = Z.

Can you crack her code?

13 1 24'

20 15 15 2 1 4 1 2 15 21 20 20 8 5 2 18 15 11 5 14

2 15 14 5. 9 7 21 5 19 19 4 5 20 5 3 20 9 22 5 23 15 18 11 3 1 14

2 5 1 16 1 9 14 9 14 20 8 5 12 5 7 19 15 13 5 20 9 13 5 19

8 1! 8 1!

1 12 9 19 15 14

Max wrote back to Alison using a code. He started at the letter J, so 1 = J and 26 = I.

Can you decipher Max's comeback?

18 3 26 10 6 5'

13 22 9 16 23 12 5 5 16. 11 25 6 10 22

18 9 22 11 25 22 19 9 22 18 2 10 14 25 22 5

16 6 12 9 22 18 21 22 11 22 20 11 26 13 22

22 15 11 9 18 6 9 21 26 5 18 26 9 22!

4 18 15

Nosy Neighbour

The Case of the
Nosy Neighbour

Did you know that babies have more than 300 bones in their bodies, but adults only have 206? Max Finder here, fact collector and Grade 7 detective. Last month I broke my leg, so I'm itching to get my cast off and to find a new mystery.

BINOCULARS ARE NOT FOR SNOOPING ON YOUR NEIGHBOURS, MAX!

BACKYARD-WATCHING IS WAY MORE FUN THAN BIRDWATCHING.

Every backyard holds a story. Mrs. Briggs's puppy elevator saved her from climbing the stairs to let her dog, Peaches, out anytime he wanted, which was every 10 minutes.

Russell Wagner's parents were going away for the weekend, and it didn't look like he'd miss them one bit.

NOBODY LIKES A NOSY NEIGHBOUR, MAX. REMEMBER, THEY KNOW WHERE YOU LIVE, TOO.

Later that night...

KRASH!

WHAT WAS THAT?

54

THIS IS GOING TO BE SO COOL!

SHH...YOU'LL WAKE THE WHOLE NEIGHBOURHOOD.

Whatever Russell was up to, I bet his parents didn't know about it.

The next evening my mom was out, so Alison and Zoe dropped by to hang out.

IT SAYS HERE, AT 8:21 PM, A SHIPMENT HAD JUST ARRIVED WHEN TWO MEN IN MASKS PULLED UP IN A WINDOWLESS VAN AND TOOK THE COMPUTERS STILL IN THEIR BOXES.

I HEARD TECH WORLD, THAT COMPUTER STORE AROUND THE CORNER, WAS ROBBED LAST NIGHT! THEY CAUGHT THE WHOLE THING ON THE SECURITY CAMERA.

MY SISTER WORKS WITH RUSSELL IN THE BOOKSTORE BESIDE TECH WORLD. HE'S ALWAYS OVER THERE TALKING ABOUT COMPUTERS.

RUSSELL GOT A BUNCH OF COMPUTERS LAST NIGHT. I BET HE'S IN ON IT.

THEN HE WOULD HAVE KNOWN ABOUT THE NEW SHIPMENT.

ROBBING A STORE IS A BIG JOB FOR A 17-YEAR-OLD. THAT BUSTED LEG HAS BROKEN YOUR MYSTERY RADAR, MAX.

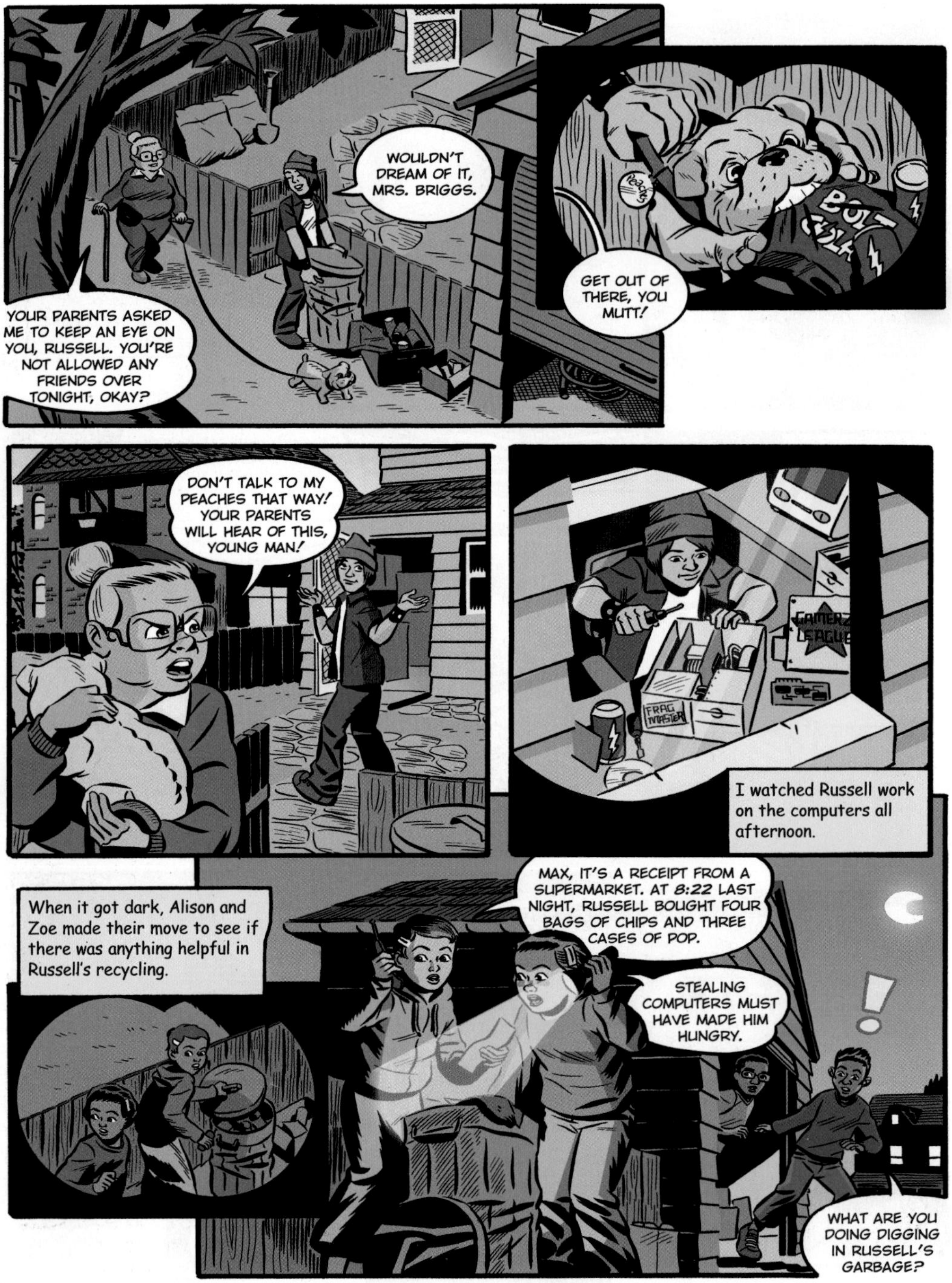
WOULDN'T DREAM OF IT, MRS. BRIGGS.
YOUR PARENTS ASKED ME TO KEEP AN EYE ON YOU, RUSSELL. YOU'RE NOT ALLOWED ANY FRIENDS OVER TONIGHT, OKAY?
PEACHES
GET OUT OF THERE, YOU MUTT!
DON'T TALK TO MY PEACHES THAT WAY! YOUR PARENTS WILL HEAR OF THIS, YOUNG MAN!
GAMERZ LEAGUE
FRAG MASTER
I watched Russell work on the computers all afternoon.
When it got dark, Alison and Zoe made their move to see if there was anything helpful in Russell's recycling.
MAX, IT'S A RECEIPT FROM A SUPERMARKET. AT 8:22 LAST NIGHT, RUSSELL BOUGHT FOUR BAGS OF CHIPS AND THREE CASES OF POP.
STEALING COMPUTERS MUST HAVE MADE HIM HUNGRY.
!
WHAT ARE YOU DOING DIGGING IN RUSSELL'S GARBAGE?

I watched in horror as Russell charged out of his house and our whole operation fell apart.

WHO ARE YOU TALKING TO ON THAT PHONE?

I SEE YOU, MAX FINDER! I'LL TEACH YOU TO SPY ON YOUR NEIGHBOURS.

The back door slammed open. Russell stormed into my house and stomped up the stairs. I was trapped.

SLAM!

POP!

RUSSELL! STOP! MAX, I KNOW THE TRUTH. I'VE FIGURED IT OUT!

Is Russell the computer thief? All the clues are here. Turn to page 78 for the solution.

57

What's It?

Max and his broken leg have been stuck in his room for days. **Can you make out what objects he's spotted out the window with his binoculars?**

1

2

PUSH-POUS

3

4

5

6

7

8

ANSWER PAGE 83

Reflection Detection

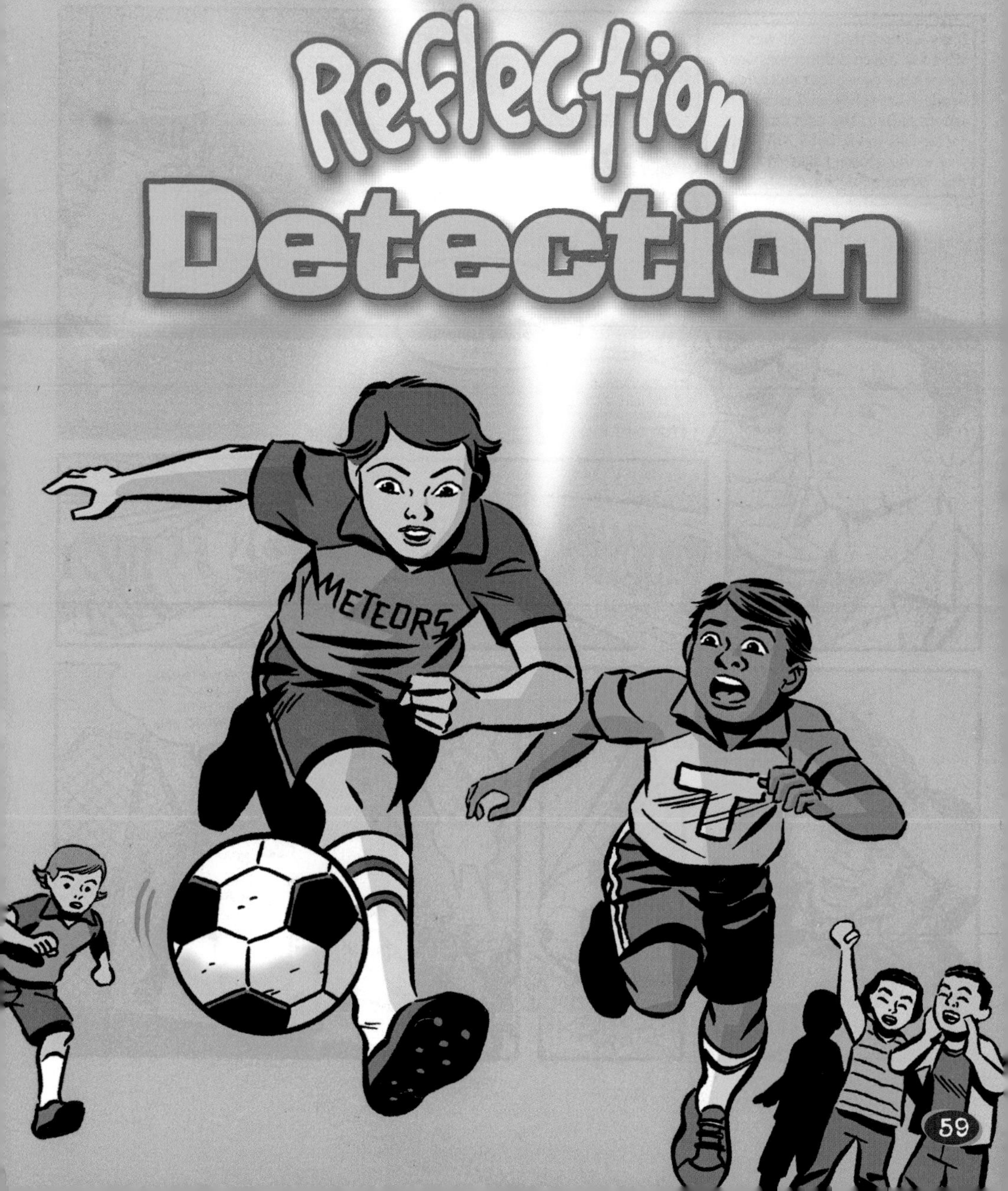
METEORS

The Case of the Reflection Detection

Did you know that soccer was played in Japan 3,000 years ago? Max Finder here, fact collector, Grade 7 detective, and sidelined soccer player. The cast came off my leg last week, but I still can't play in the season finals against the Twindale Tornadoes.

I KNOW I WENT TO TWINDALE LAST YEAR, MAX, BUT I WANT THE MEADOWS METEORS TO WIN!

THAT'S GOING TO BE TOUGH, ZOE, IF BASHER DOESN'T STOP THIS SHOT.

POOMP!

GAH! MY EYES!

YAAY!

SWISH!

SOMETHING FLASHED IN MY EYES. IT BLINDED ME!

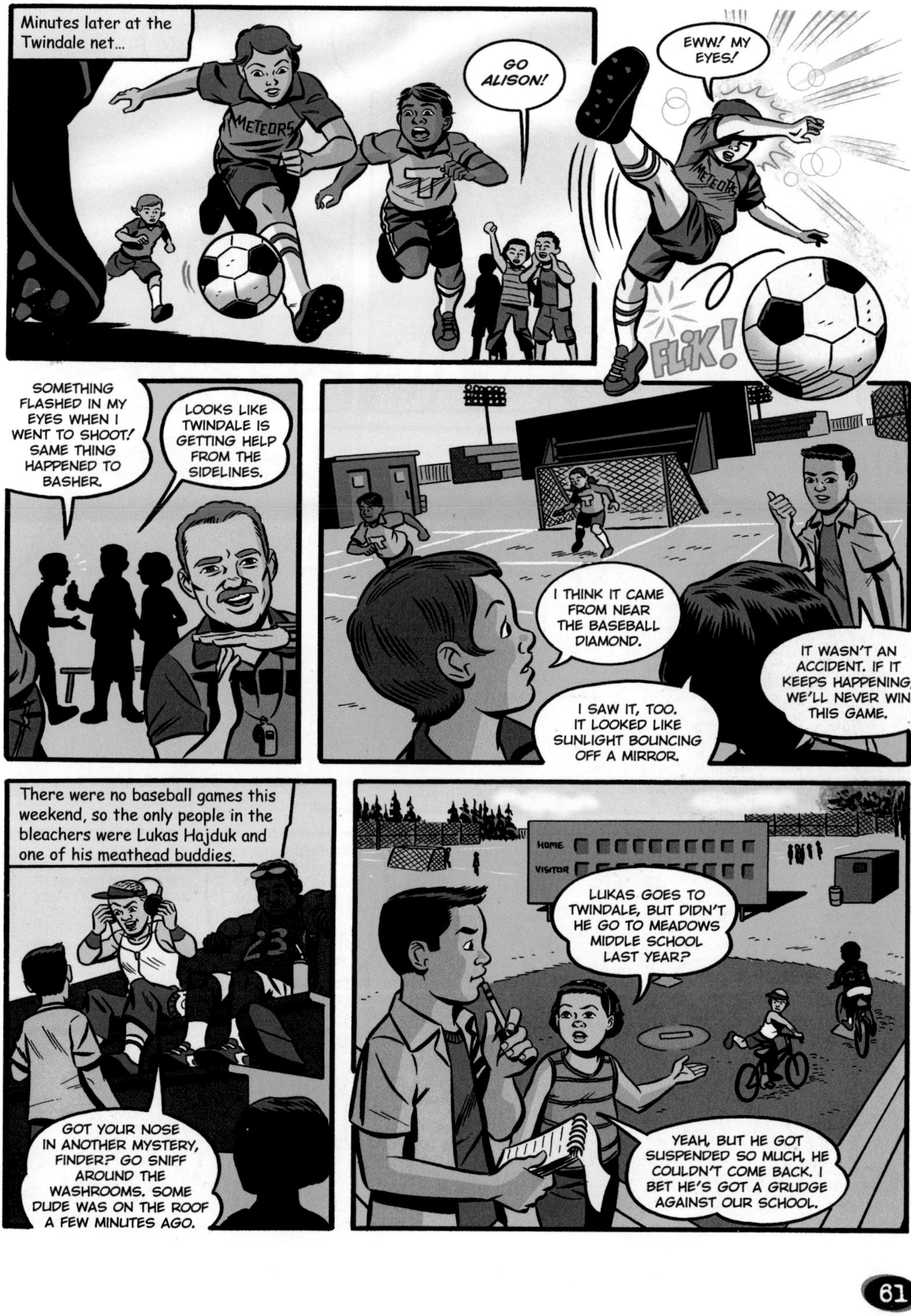
Minutes later at the Twindale net...
GO ALISON!
EWW! MY EYES!
FLIK!
SOMETHING FLASHED IN MY EYES WHEN I WENT TO SHOOT! SAME THING HAPPENED TO BASHER.
LOOKS LIKE TWINDALE IS GETTING HELP FROM THE SIDELINES.
I THINK IT CAME FROM NEAR THE BASEBALL DIAMOND.
I SAW IT, TOO. IT LOOKED LIKE SUNLIGHT BOUNCING OFF A MIRROR.
IT WASN'T AN ACCIDENT. IF IT KEEPS HAPPENING, WE'LL NEVER WIN THIS GAME.
There were no baseball games this weekend, so the only people in the bleachers were Lukas Hajduk and one of his meathead buddies.
GOT YOUR NOSE IN ANOTHER MYSTERY, FINDER? GO SNIFF AROUND THE WASHROOMS. SOME DUDE WAS ON THE ROOF A FEW MINUTES AGO.
HOME
VISITOR
LUKAS GOES TO TWINDALE, BUT DIDN'T HE GO TO MEADOWS MIDDLE SCHOOL LAST YEAR?
YEAH, BUT HE GOT SUSPENDED SO MUCH, HE COULDN'T COME BACK. I BET HE'S GOT A GRUDGE AGAINST OUR SCHOOL.

As we headed back to the soccer field, former Meteors star, Kate Yoon, whizzed by on her bike.

HEY, KATE! TOO BAD YOU QUIT THE SOCCER TEAM. WE COULD REALLY USE YOU OUT THERE TODAY.

FORGET IT MAX. SOCCER IS FOR WIMPS.

THAT'S WEIRD. I THOUGHT KATE LOVED SOCCER.

LOOK! IT'S THE MIRROR FLASHER!

HEY, YOU! GET DOWN FROM THERE!

ZOE, STOP!

GAH!

THUDD!

YOU'RE MR. HUCKLE. YOU COACHED THE TWINDALE TORNADOES LAST YEAR!

WHEN MR. HUCKLE COACHED THE TORNADOES THEY LOST EVERY GAME. EVEN THOUGH HE WAS FIRED, HE'S STILL OBSESSED WITH WINNING.

A VICTORY WOULD MAKE HIS DREAMS COME TRUE. AND THE ROOF WOULD BE A PERFECT HIDING SPOT FOR SHINING THE MIRROR.

I WAS TRYING TO GET A BETTER VIEW OF THE GAME. I SAW A KID IN BLUE SHORTS CLIMB ONTO A MOUNTAIN BIKE TO GET ON THE ROOF. I FIGURED I'D GIVE IT A TRY.

At halftime our team was down by a goal. We filled Zoe's sister, Andrea, and Alison in on our investigation.

KATE'S HAD A GRUDGE AGAINST THE SOCCER TEAM SINCE SHE HAD TO QUIT TO IMPROVE HER GRADES.

MY LAST YEAR AT TWINDALE I HAD MR. HUCKLE FOR SCIENCE. HE TAUGHT US HOW MIRRORS REFLECT LIGHT.

Not long into the second half...

AHH!

LET'S GO!

THIS TIME IT CAME FROM THAT SNACK BAR!

The busy snack bar was the perfect place for the mirror flasher to hide out.

SNACK BAR

YOU'D NEED TO BE HIGH UP TO GET A CLEAR SHOT OF THE SOCCER FIELD FROM HERE.

I DON'T SEE THE MIRROR FLASHER AROUND HERE.

EXACTLY. GET BACK IN THE GAME, ALISON. I KNOW WHO IS BLINDING THE PLAYERS.

Who is blinding the soccer players? Turn to page 79 to find out.

forensics Quiz

Test your C.S.I. (that's crime scene investigation) skills with the questions below.

	True	False
1. There are three main types of fingerprints. They're called arch, loop, and globular.	☐	☐
2. Detectives and forensic scientists can use toe prints or lip prints to identify someone.	☐	☐
3. The fingerprint brush that detectives use to dust for prints may be made from squirrel hair.	☐	☐
4. To lift hair and fibres from surfaces, detectives often use a comb.	☐	☐
5. Detectives often make a cast, or mould, of a footprint to preserve their find, in case they need it later.	☐	☐
6. By examining a strand of hair, scientists can help a detective determine if the person was male or female.	☐	☐
7. Detectives may use a special vacuum cleaner to suck up evidence at a crime scene.	☐	☐
8. By looking closely at an imprint made by a foot inside a sneaker, detectives can match it to the actual foot.	☐	☐
9. At crime scenes, investigators bring their own super-bright lights so they don't miss any clues.	☐	☐
10. By examining someone's handwriting, detectives can figure out whether the person is left-handed or right-handed.	☐	☐

ANSWER PAGE 83

Summer Sinker

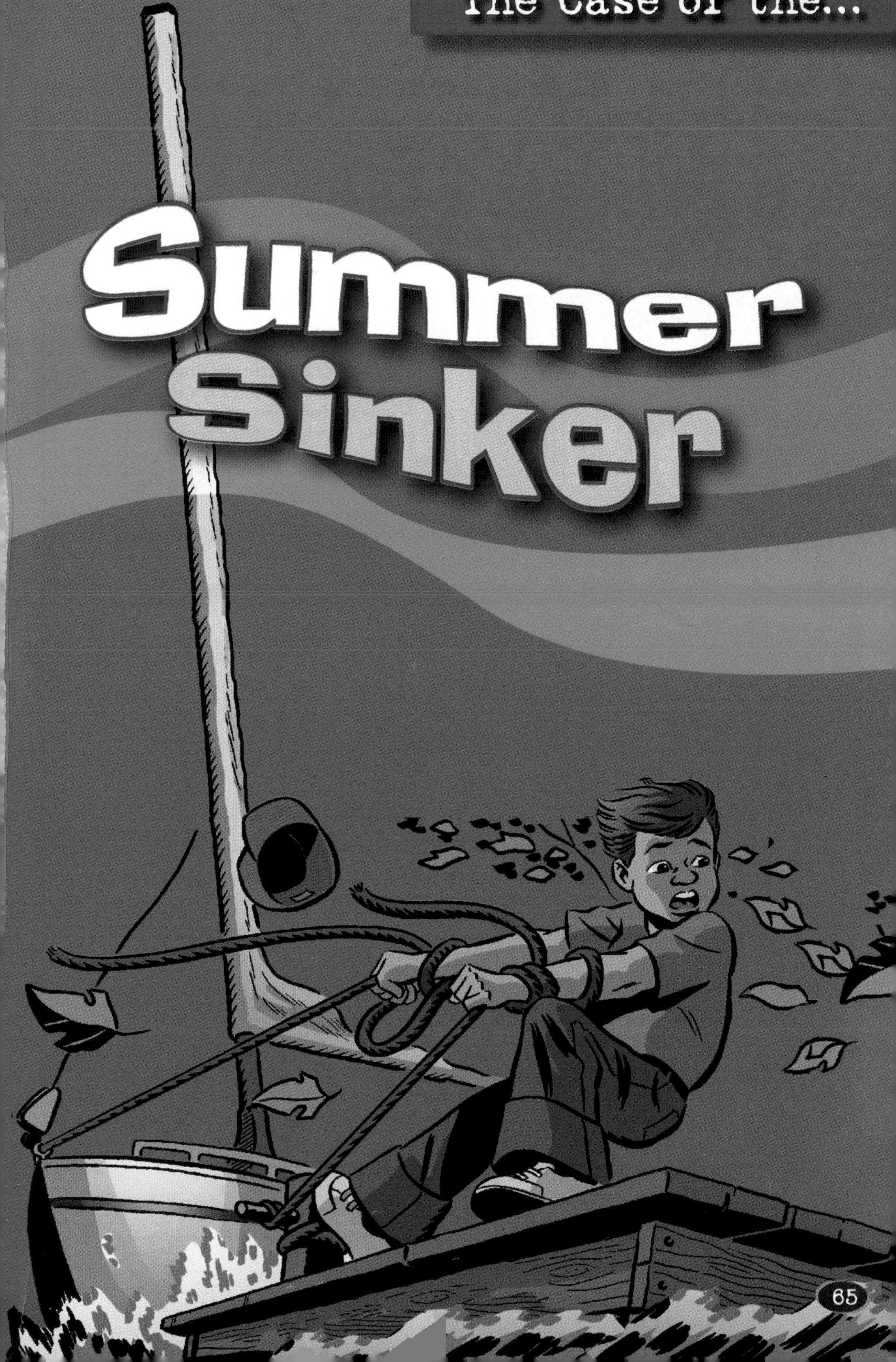

The Case of the
Summer Sinker

Did you know the katydid grasshopper has ears in its legs? Max Finder here, fact collector and Grade 7 detective. Alison and I are visiting her grandfather at his cottage on Trout Lake. He's been coming here since he was a boy. Today, all his old friends are here for some barbecue fun.

MYSTERY ALERT, MAX!

cho

The chip-hound is Cory Klein and the girl is Amanda Shaw. They spend the summer at the lake. Alison was looking at an old scrapbook from the 1950s, when Grandpa Santos was a kid.

CHECK THIS OUT.

Boat Sinker Revealed!

"12-year-old Danny Santos blamed for marina mischief"

Tragedy struck the Trout Lake marina last night. Four sailboats had their plugs, known as bungs, removed, sending some of the boats to the bottom of the lake. A red baseball cap, bearing the name "Danny Santos," was found inside one of the sunken boats leading police to conclude that the boy was behind the sinkings. Two of the boats were saved by the quick thinking of Warren

Klein, also 12 years old. The son of the marina owner heroically jumped into the water and replaced the bungs to stop the boats from sinking.

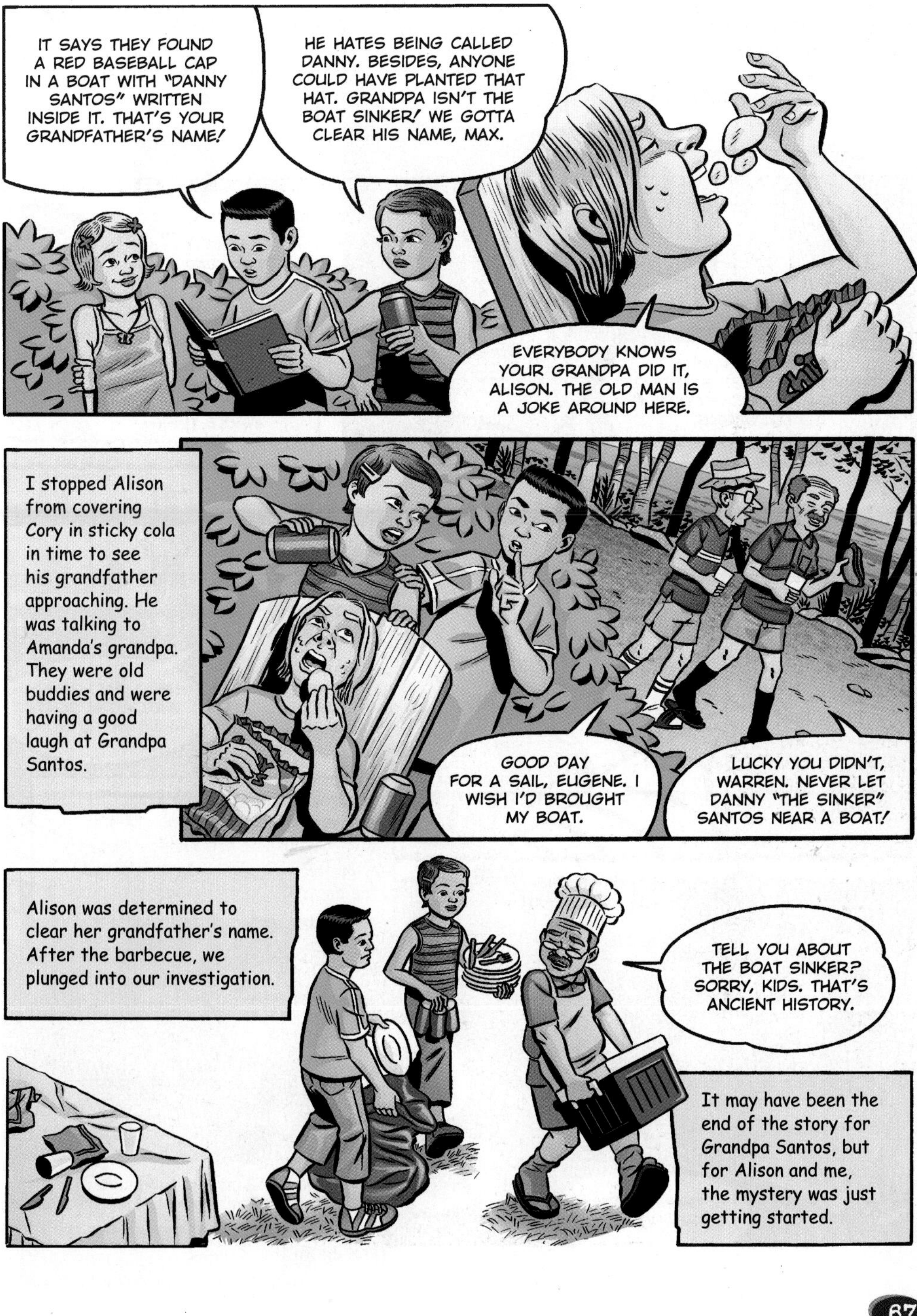
IT SAYS THEY FOUND A RED BASEBALL CAP IN A BOAT WITH "DANNY SANTOS" WRITTEN INSIDE IT. THAT'S YOUR GRANDFATHER'S NAME!
HE HATES BEING CALLED DANNY. BESIDES, ANYONE COULD HAVE PLANTED THAT HAT. GRANDPA ISN'T THE BOAT SINKER! WE GOTTA CLEAR HIS NAME, MAX.
EVERYBODY KNOWS YOUR GRANDPA DID IT, ALISON. THE OLD MAN IS A JOKE AROUND HERE.
I stopped Alison from covering Cory in sticky cola in time to see his grandfather approaching. He was talking to Amanda's grandpa. They were old buddies and were having a good laugh at Grandpa Santos.
GOOD DAY FOR A SAIL, EUGENE. I WISH I'D BROUGHT MY BOAT.
LUCKY YOU DIDN'T, WARREN. NEVER LET DANNY "THE SINKER" SANTOS NEAR A BOAT!
Alison was determined to clear her grandfather's name. After the barbecue, we plunged into our investigation.
TELL YOU ABOUT THE BOAT SINKER? SORRY, KIDS. THAT'S ANCIENT HISTORY.
It may have been the end of the story for Grandpa Santos, but for Alison and me, the mystery was just getting started.

The next day, we headed to the library. The boat sinkings made all the papers around Trout Lake that summer. The sinker struck during the July 1 fireworks.

THE ENTIRE TOWN WAS AT THE BEACH WATCHING THE FIREWORKS.

Margaret Kim, the librarian, is friends with Grandpa Santos. She remembered the boat sinkings—and that red baseball cap.

ONE WITNESS SAW A SKINNY KID IN A RED BASEBALL CAP ON THE DOCK DURING THE FIREWORKS.

YOUR GRANDPA LOST THAT CAP BEFORE THE SINKING. I SAW THE WHOLE THING.

A week before the sinkings, I was at the marina. Dan was visiting his buddy Eugene, who worked there with Warren. Warren's dad owned the marina and the restaurant in town.

DAN, WE'RE OFF TO THE BEACH WHILE MY DAD IS AT LUNCH.

BE A PAL, DANNY. WATCH THE BOATS WHILE WE'RE GONE!

Dan would do anything to avoid swimming. He hated taking off his shirt because he felt chubby. But when the wind picked up, Dan saved the boats.

WHERE THE HECK ARE WARREN AND EUGENE?

THEY WENT SWIMMING, SIR!

Mr. Klein fired Eugene and made Warren wash the dishes in his restaurant. Both boys blamed Dan for telling on them.

After lunch, we paid a visit to Eugene. He and Warren had a motive, but did they have an alibi? We asked him where he was when the boat sinker struck.

I REMEMBER IT WELL. I WAS WITH MARGARET AND WARREN ON THE BEACH WATCHING THE FIREWORKS.

I watched the whole show. Warren had to go work in the kitchen, and your grandfather showed up just as the fireworks were ending.

EUGENE, YOU GOOF. YOU TOLD ME YOU'D ALL BE AT YOUR COTTAGE!

THAT'S RUBBISH, DANNY! MY COTTAGE IS AT THE FAR END OF THE LAKE. YOU CAN'T SEE THE FIREWORKS FROM THERE.

Storytelling really took it out of Eugene. After a few questions, he snored like we weren't even there. A good detective never turns down the chance to snoop, so we snuck into Eugene's cottage. Our snooping paid off.

HEY! WHAT ARE YOU GUYS DOING?

YOUR GRANDPA AND EUGENE WERE BEST BUDDIES, WEREN'T THEY?

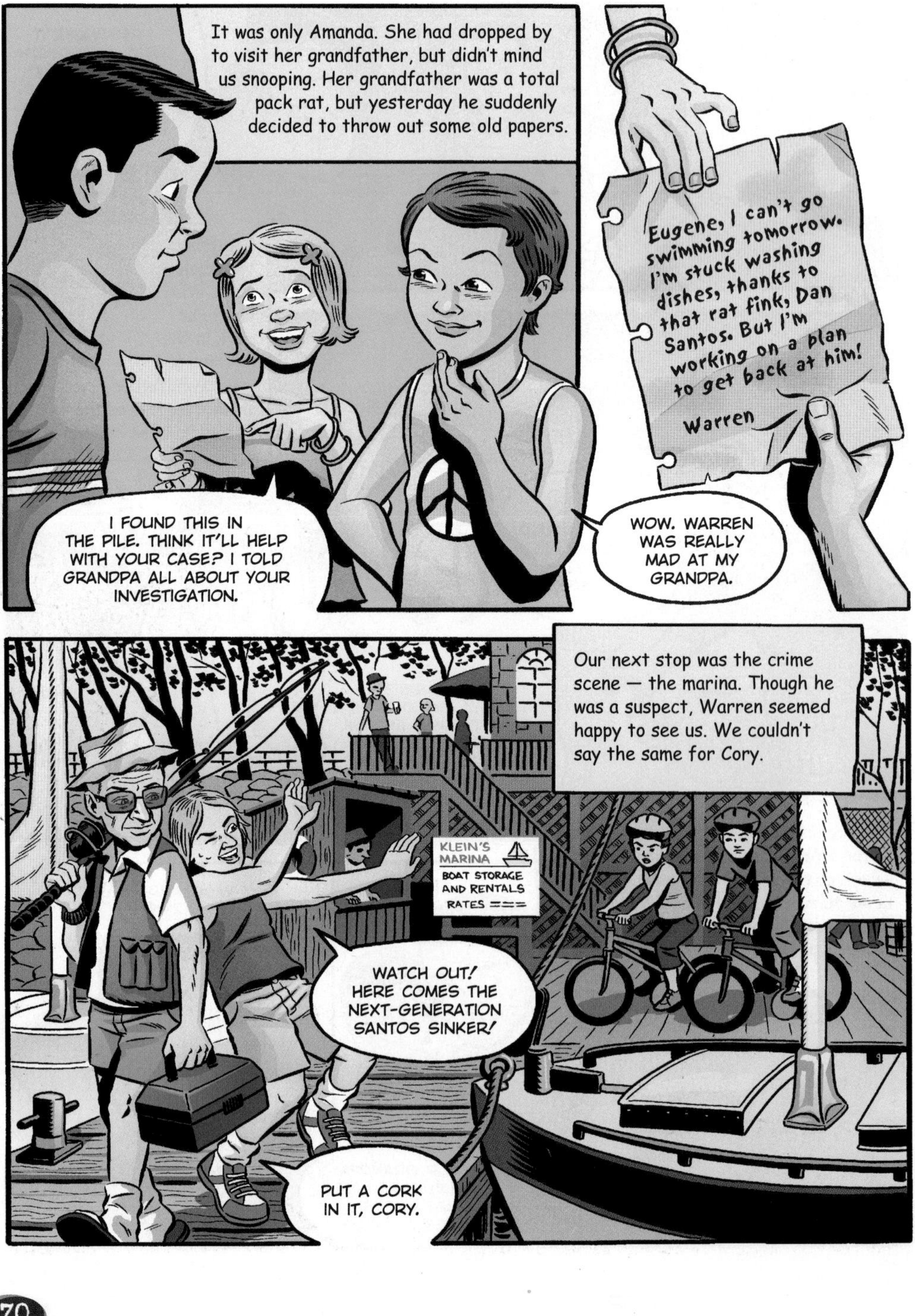
It was only Amanda. She had dropped by to visit her grandfather, but didn't mind us snooping. Her grandfather was a total pack rat, but yesterday he suddenly decided to throw out some old papers.
Eugene, I can't go swimming tomorrow. I'm stuck washing dishes, thanks to that rat fink, Dan Santos. But I'm working on a plan to get back at him!
Warren
I FOUND THIS IN THE PILE. THINK IT'LL HELP WITH YOUR CASE? I TOLD GRANDPA ALL ABOUT YOUR INVESTIGATION.
WOW. WARREN WAS REALLY MAD AT MY GRANDPA.
Our next stop was the crime scene — the marina. Though he was a suspect, Warren seemed happy to see us. We couldn't say the same for Cory.
KLEIN'S MARINA
BOAT STORAGE AND RENTALS
RATES
WATCH OUT! HERE COMES THE NEXT-GENERATION SANTOS SINKER!
PUT A CORK IN IT, CORY.

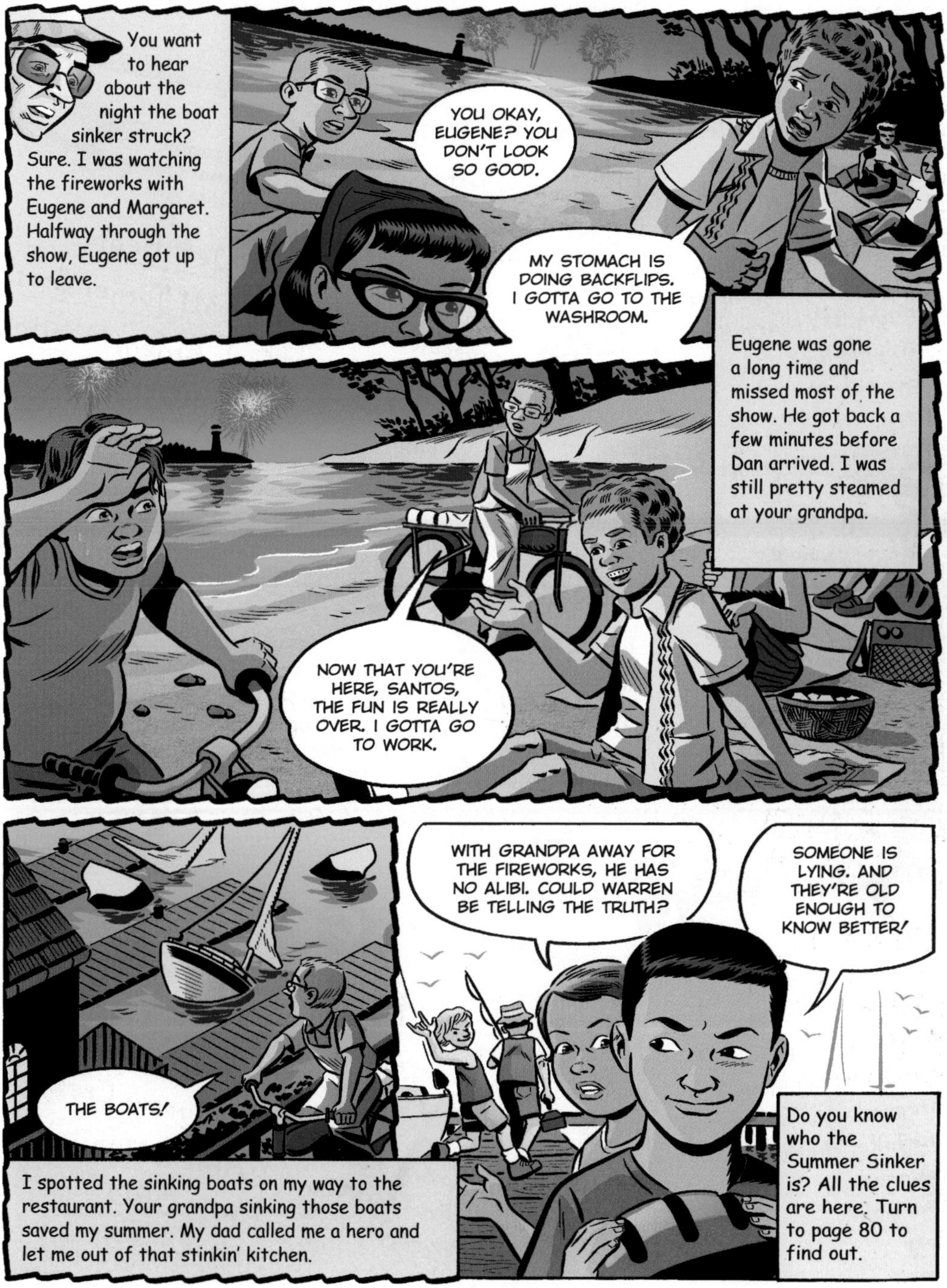
You want to hear about the night the boat sinker struck? Sure. I was watching the fireworks with Eugene and Margaret. Halfway through the show, Eugene got up to leave.
YOU OKAY, EUGENE? YOU DON'T LOOK SO GOOD.
MY STOMACH IS DOING BACKFLIPS. I GOTTA GO TO THE WASHROOM.
Eugene was gone a long time and missed most of the show. He got back a few minutes before Dan arrived. I was still pretty steamed at your grandpa.
NOW THAT YOU'RE HERE, SANTOS, THE FUN IS REALLY OVER. I GOTTA GO TO WORK.
THE BOATS!
I spotted the sinking boats on my way to the restaurant. Your grandpa sinking those boats saved my summer. My dad called me a hero and let me out of that stinkin' kitchen.
WITH GRANDPA AWAY FOR THE FIREWORKS, HE HAS NO ALIBI. COULD WARREN BE TELLING THE TRUTH?
SOMEONE IS LYING. AND THEY'RE OLD ENOUGH TO KNOW BETTER!
Do you know who the Summer Sinker is? All the clues are here. Turn to page 80 to find out.

Postcard Scramble

Cory is spending his summer vacation at Trout Lake. He's been sending postcards to his friend, Jeff Bean, telling him about all the fun he's having. **Can you put the postcards in the correct order?**

a

Hey Jeff,
Wakeboarding rules. I'm a natural. Amanda showed me "the big rock" on the other side of the lake. She says we're going to jump off it soon. It's scary-high. Wish me luck.
Your pal,
Cory

Beautiful Trout Lake
Catch the 'big one'

Jeff Bean
311 Turner Cres.,
Arden, Manitoba
R0J 0B0

b

Hey Jeff,
I just arrived but so far Trout Lake is wicked. First thing I want to try is wakeboarding. Fishing is supposed to be good, too. I've got all summer to try my luck.
Your pal,
Cory

51

Beautiful Trout Lake
Catch the 'big one'

Jeff Bean
311 Turner Cres.,
Arden, Manitoba
R0J 0B0

c

Hey Jeff,
We had a huge bonfire last night. It was cool to hang out by the fire. Especially because there were bats swooping down at our heads. I can't believe summer's almost over.
Your pal,
Cory

Beautiful Trout Lake
Catch the 'big one'

Jeff Bean
311 Turner
Arden, M
R0J 0B0

d

Hey Jeff,
We finally jumped off "the big rock" today. Man, it was scary — but amazing. And then I actually found my sunglasses. They washed up on shore. Can you believe that? The best day yet!
Your pal,
Cory

Beautiful Trout Lake
Catch the 'big one'

Jeff Bean
311 Turner Cres.,
Ard
nitoba

e

Hey Jeff,
Went fishing today. Pretty boring after wakeboarding. I didn't catch a thing. And, I dropped my sunglasses in the lake. They're gone for good.
Your pal,
Cory

Je
311
Ard
R0J

f

Hey Jeff,
Gave the fishing thing another chance. I left my sunglasses at the cottage this time... just in case! Still no trout. Having a bonfire tomorrow. I wish you could be here!
Your pal,
Cory

51

Beautiful Trout Lake
Catch the 'big one'

Jeff Bean
311 Turner Cres.,
Arden, Manitoba
R0J 0B0

ANSWER PAGE 83

Who? what? when? Where? how? why?

Case Solutions

The Case of the Trail Trap
(page 11)

Who made the trap to trip Andrea?
- **Ethan Webster**. Ethan was scared of losing his spot as the school's top cross-country runner. So he sawed sticks with Josh's Swiss Army knife to make a trap that would hurt Andrea and put her out of the upcoming race.

How did Max solve the case?
- Ethan was the only person at school who knew that Shawna had called Andrea a traitor.
- Max and Alison saw Ethan return the Swiss Army knife to Josh.
- Ethan said he was too ill to go running with Andrea on the morning she found the trap. But Josh said that he and Ethan had played basketball "yesterday morning" — the same day Andrea found the trap.
- Josh also told the detectives that Ethan complained about Andrea.
- Further study of Zoe's footprint mould showed it was made from Jessica's riding boot. She walked around the trap because her pony sensed something was wrong on the trail and wouldn't walk forward. The pony knew the trap was there even if Jessica didn't!

Conclusion
When faced with the evidence, Ethan confessed to setting the trap. As a punishment, he wasn't allowed to run in the weekend's big race. Andrea won the race and easily beat Ethan's best time.

The Case of the Model Plane Mess-up
(page 17)

Who crashed Alex's plane?
- **Katlyn Rodriguez**. Katlyn didn't want to spend her Saturday afternoon flying model planes, so she took Alex's pieces of wildberry gum from his coat pocket, chewed them, and wedged them into the wings of the plane. Katlyn didn't know much about planes but she hoped that would be enough to ground Alex for the day and get her to the movie theatre.

How did Alison solve the case?
- Although she denied chewing any of the wildberry gum, Katlyn had a blue tongue. (She stuck it out when they were all walking home.)
- Crystal and Katlyn helped prepare Alex's plane for flight, but Crystal was still chewing her piece of gum after the crash. She blew a bubble when Stuart was looking at the damaged wing.
- Nicholas had chewed his gum but hadn't spoken to Alex for a month, so he didn't get near enough to the plane to sabotage it.

Case Solutions

- Stuart hadn't even chewed his gum when Max and Alison spoke to him.
- Alison spotted Katlyn and Alex at the theatre. That reminded Alison that Katlyn didn't want to go flying in the first place. She wanted to go to the movies instead.

Conclusion

Max and Alison confronted Katlyn just before Alex bought the movie tickets. Katlyn confessed to wedging gum into the wing of her brother's plane and apologized. Instead of spending the money on a movie, Katlyn and Alex bought new parts for the crashed plane. They spent the afternoon fixing the plane and getting it ready for one last flight before the winter snows arrived.

The Case of the Lucky Skates

(page 23)

Who stole Tony's skates?

- **Lorrisa Swart**. She didn't want Tony to beat her brother Simon's high-scoring record. So she took Tony's lucky skates, knowing it would make him miss the game.

Where were the lucky skates hidden?

- Behind the arena, in the snow pile created by the Zamboni.

How did Alison solve the case?

- Doug Chang said Lorrisa knocked over the garbage can with a blue hockey bag. But Alison saw Basher looking through Lorrisa's green bag. The blue bag was Tony's. (Basher was looking for skate laces.)
- Lorrisa hid in the girls' washroom to take Tony's skates from his bag. Tony's skate guard fell from the bag when Lorrisa knocked over the garbage on her way into the washroom.
- Alison was suspicious about the open washroom window. As she talked to Max from the window, she noticed the freshly dumped snow directly below her.
- Lorrisa threw Tony's skates out the window. She knew they'd be covered when the Zamboni dumped its load of snow.

Conclusion

Tony dug his skates out of the snow in time for the faceoff. The Minotaurs won, but Tony only tied Simon's record. After the game, Lorrisa confessed. Tony was just happy to have his skates back and didn't hold a grudge. He even promised to pass the puck more.

Case Solutions

The Case of the Angry Anchorman

(page 29)

Who stole Bull's wig?
- **Ursula Curtis**. Ursula was tired of her father working on the late news. She thought if she could get Max's mom in trouble, Bull would switch her shift with her father's and bring him back to the five o'clock news. Then Ursula would see more of him.

Where is the wig?
- It's in the wastebasket, buried under the pile of paper napkins.

How did Max and Alison solve the case?
- Ursula was alone with Deb, Bull, and the wig. She had the opportunity to steal it.
- Fran said the wig was gone when she walked into the dressing room. Ursula lied when she said the wig was on the stand when she left the makeup room.
- Ursula hid the wig under her zipped-up winter coat.
- Ursula complained about never seeing her father because he worked on the late news. That gave her a motive to get Bull mad at Max's mom.
- There wasn't a drop of juice on the table but Ursula said she made a big mess. She was lying to justify using so many paper napkins.

Conclusion

Ursula admitted to stealing the wig. She got the idea when she saw Bull get angry at Kyle. Bull pulled his wig out of the garbage and read the five o'clock news. Ursula was not allowed to go on TV to present the charity money. The news went off without a hitch, except for when Bull O'Wiley sat in the large wad of bubble gum Kyle stuck on his TV studio seat. The joker was later heard saying, "Payback can be sticky, but it's always sweet."

The Case of the Missing Manga

(page 35)

Who stole Sarah's sketchbook?
- **Crystal Diallo**. Crystal wasn't interested in the Takahashi manga page. She wanted her drawing to be used for the cover of the school's comic book. With Sarah's drawing missing, hers would be used.

How did Max solve the case?
- Crystal said she didn't see anything because she was posing for photos with Sarah and Kengo Takahashi. But she left them to get a headband out of her bag, which was right beside Sarah's bag. That's when she grabbed Jake's sketchbook and made the switch.
- Crystal was lying about her mom being off work. Sarah's sketchbook was hidden in Crystal's bag and she wanted to get home before anyone saw it.

Case Solutions

Conclusion

Crystal admitted to switching the sketchbooks. She hoped that everyone would look for the manga page and not realize that Sarah's cover art was the real target. Crystal returned Sarah's sketchbook just in time to get Sarah's drawing on the cover of the comic. The comic was a hit, and Sarah agreed to use Crystal's drawing for the cover on the second issue.

The Case of the Elvis Prankster

(page 41)

Who is the Elvis prankster?

- **Chester Winfield**. Chester wanted to compete in the Grand Ballroom so badly that he dressed up like Elvis and pulled the pranks. He was hoping the Elvis convention would be blamed and get kicked out of the hotel, freeing the ballroom for the dog show.

How did Max solve the case?

- When Max and Eric talked to Chester, he was holding his dog in the white Elvis cape. That's why there was red hair on the cape in the hotel room.
- The chef said the sandwich buyer was a man, so it couldn't have been Nicole.

- Chester lied about who delivered the peanut butter sandwiches. The dog show woman said that Chester wasn't there when it happened. That's because he was disguised as Elvis delivering the sandwiches!
- Max heard Nicole giving Tinkerbell a bath just before the Elvis prankster got dressed. So she couldn't be the prankster.
- Witnesses saw an Elvis in a white cape pull the pranks — Alvin was wearing a black leather jacket. He couldn't be the prankster either.

Conclusion

Chester admitted to pulling the Elvis pranks. He was kicked out of the dog show and the Elvis competition went ahead as planned. Eric had a great performance and became the new Elvis champion.

Case Solutions

The Case of the Gander River Grudge

(page 47)

Who is making the geese sick?
• **Kristen Taylor**. Kristen wanted the geese away from her flowers. She covered the river banks with soybeans because she knew the geese would all go there to eat the beans and leave her flowers alone.

How did Max solve the case?
• There were soybeans scattered in the back of Kristen's electric cart.
• Zack was using chemicals on the golf course, but Becca didn't find any chemicals on the soybeans, so Zack wasn't the culprit.
• Although he couldn't see who knocked him down, Max knew that it could not have been Zack because he was on the other side of the river. It also wasn't Josh or his dad because they were fishing under the bridge. That only left Kristen.
• Max heard a low hum right after he fell down the river bank. It was the sound of an electric cart. It was Kristen driving away after crashing into Max and Alison.

Conclusion
Kristen confessed to feeding soybeans to the geese. She didn't know that the beans would make the birds sick. They kept the geese away from her flowers and that's all that mattered to Kristen, so she kept spreading them along the river. She agreed to clean them off the banks and think of a safer way to keep the geese away from her flowers. The sick geese made a full recovery. Max wasn't so lucky. He broke his leg when Kristen knocked him down. Now he's got a cast on his leg and he's stuck at home.

The Case of the Nosy Neighbour

(page 53)

Did Russell rob the computer store?
No, but he was up to something sneaky. Although his parents told him not to have any friends over, Russell was planning to have a computer game party. Russell borrowed his friends' computers and was hooking them all up so they could play games together. Russell knew that Mrs. Briggs was keeping an eye on him, so he snuck the computers into his house at night.

How did Alison solve the case?
• The van that Max saw did not match the description of the van caught on the computer store's surveillance camera.

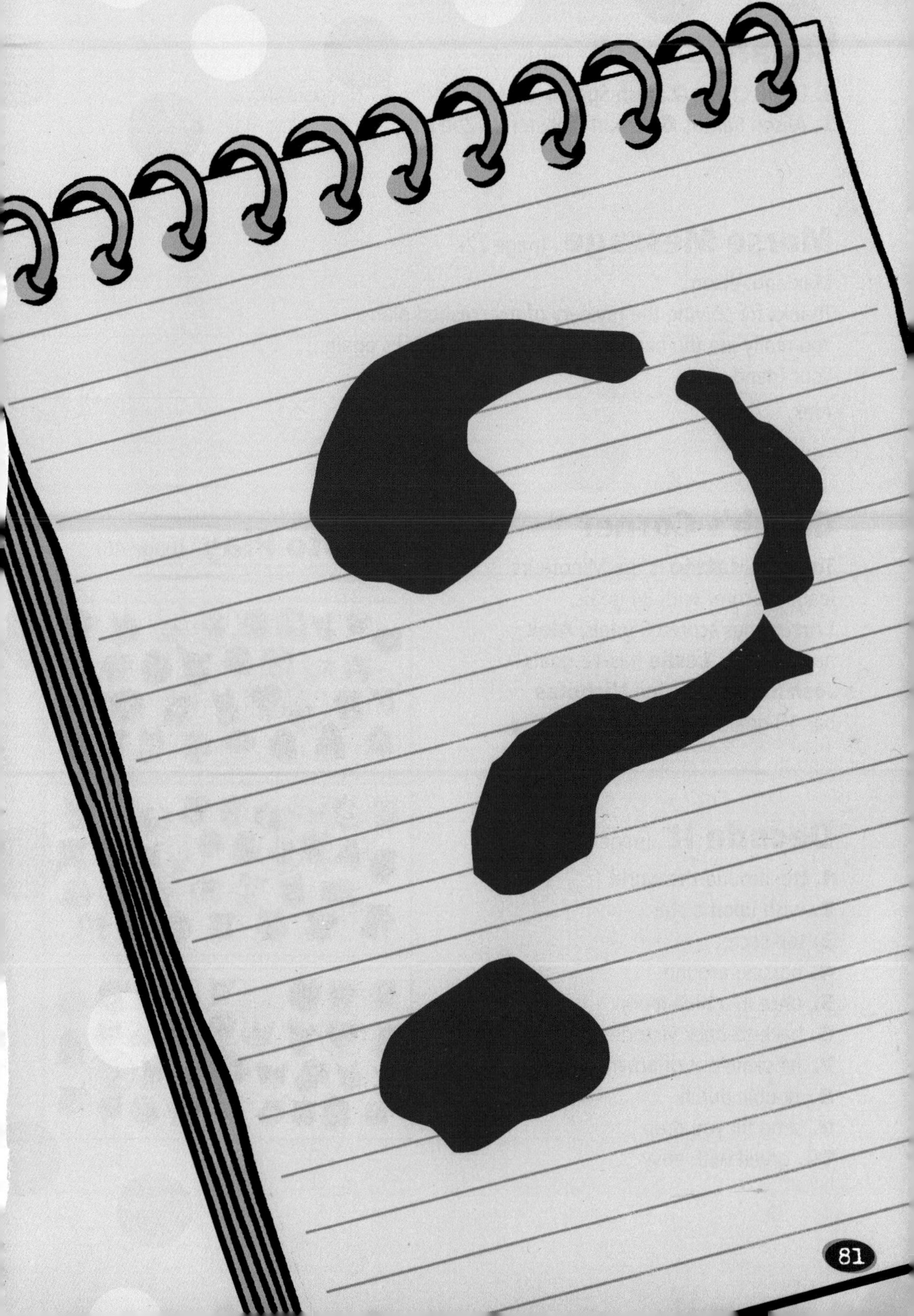

Square Search (page 16)

1. Leslie Chang **2.** Josh Spodek **3.** Max Finder **4.** Nanda Kanwar
5. Alison Santos **6.** Ethan Webster **7.** Zoe Palgrave **8.** Lukas Hajduk

Morse Message (page 22)

Max and Alison:
Thanks for solving the mystery of my crashed plane.
You really are the best detectives around. Thanks again.
Your friend,
Alex

Coach's Corner (page 28)

Tony DeMatteo is the Minotaurs' leading scorer with 34 goals. **Lorrisa** has scored 6 goals, **Alex** has 17 goals, **Leslie** has 12 goals, **Josh** has 6 goals, and **Nicholas** has 15 goals.

Photo Play (page 46)

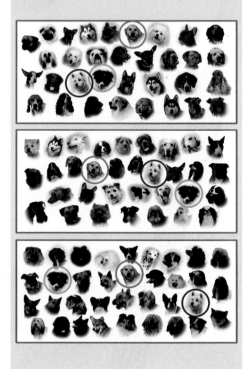

Decode It (page 40)

1. trip around the world
2. wish upon a star
3. top secret
4. horsing around
5. once in a blue moon
6. back-to-back victories
7. he came out of nowhere
8. double dutch
9. shop till you drop
10. green with envy

Cast Code (page 52)

Alison's message:
Max,
Too bad about the broken bone.
I guess detective work can be a
pain in the leg sometimes.
Ha! Ha!
Alison

Max's message:
Alison,
Very funny. Those are the
breaks when you're a detective
extraordinaire!
Max

What's It:

(page 58)

1. fire hydrant
2. mailbox
3. line on road
4. garden hose
5. car
6. skateboard
7. basketball
8. cat

Forensics Quiz (page 64)

1. False — They are arch, loop, and whorl.
2. True — They can also use things like palm prints, footprints, and bite marks.
3. True.
4. False — They often use clear tape.
5. True.
6. False — Strands of hair do not contain DNA. But if scientists find a hair root they can tell if the person is male or female.
7. True — A forensic vacuum can suck up things like fibre, paint, and glass.
8. True.
9. True.
10. False — But scientists are working on it.

Postcard Scramble

(page 72)

b
a
e
d
f
c

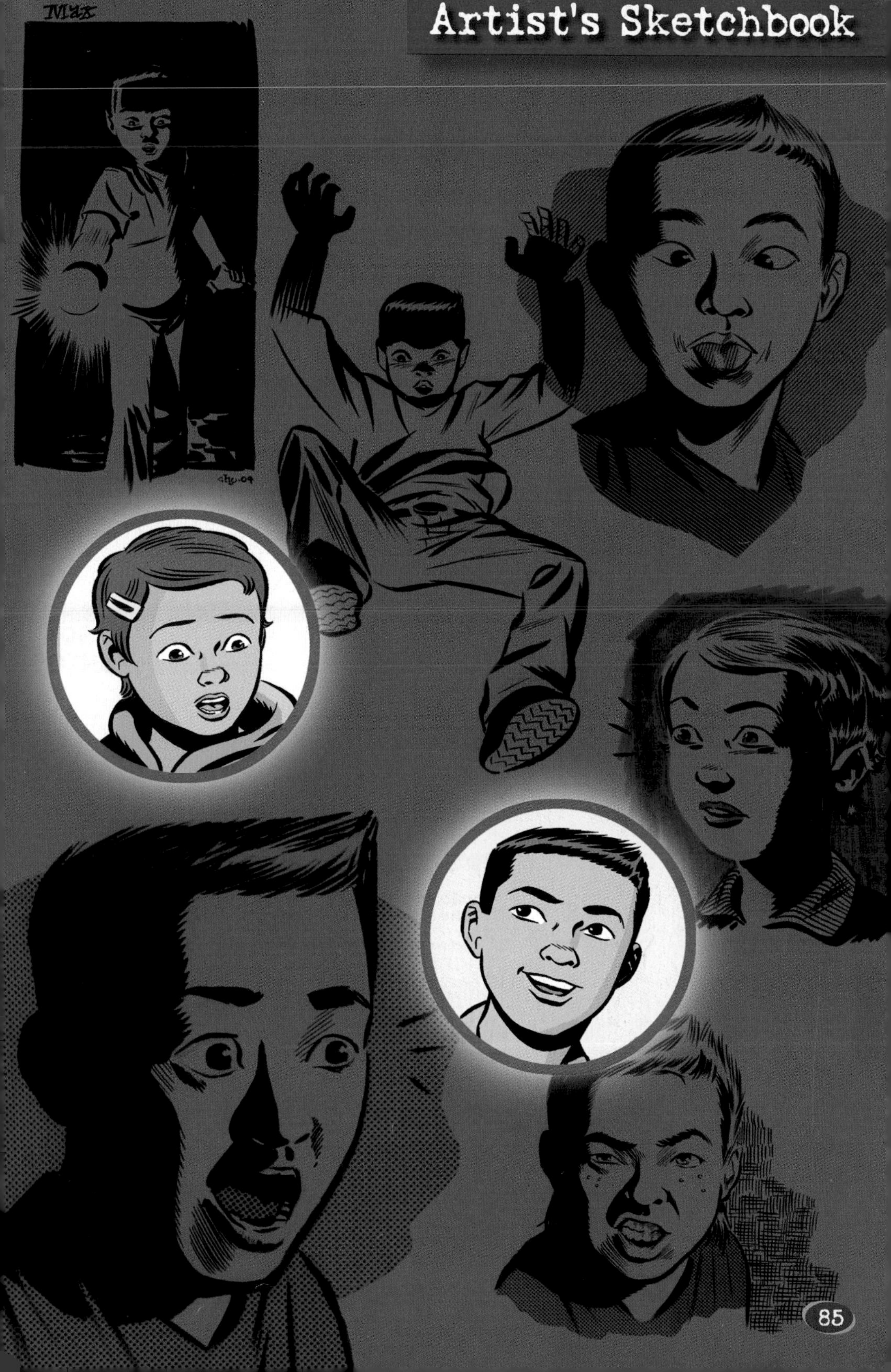
Max

Max and Alison Come to Life

Peek into illustrator Michael Cho's sketchbook and
see some of the first-ever drawings of Max and Alison.

My very first
MAX FINDER
DRAWING!
cho

My very first
ALISON SANTOS
DRAWING!
cho

MAX
FINDER

ALISON
SANTOS

Max & Alison

CHARACTER
STUDIES
&
ATTITUDES

cho

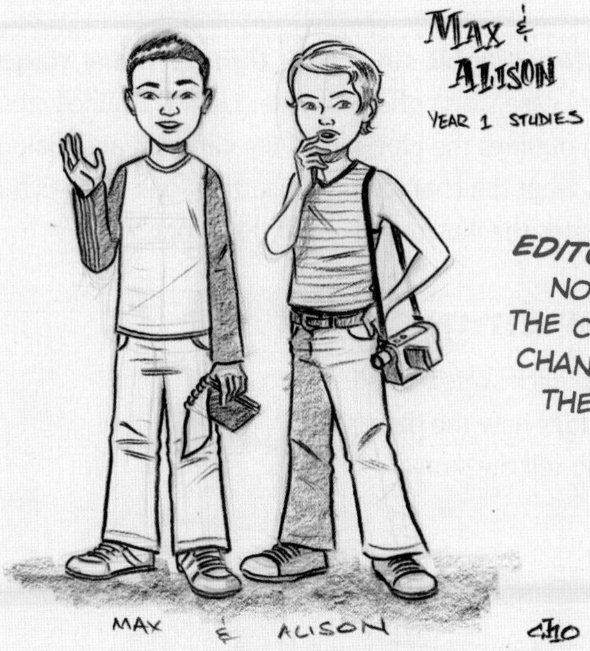
MAX & ALISON
YEAR 1 STUDIES
MAX & ALISON
CHO

EDITOR'S NOTE:
NOTICE HOW THE CHARACTERS CHANGED OVER THE YEARS.

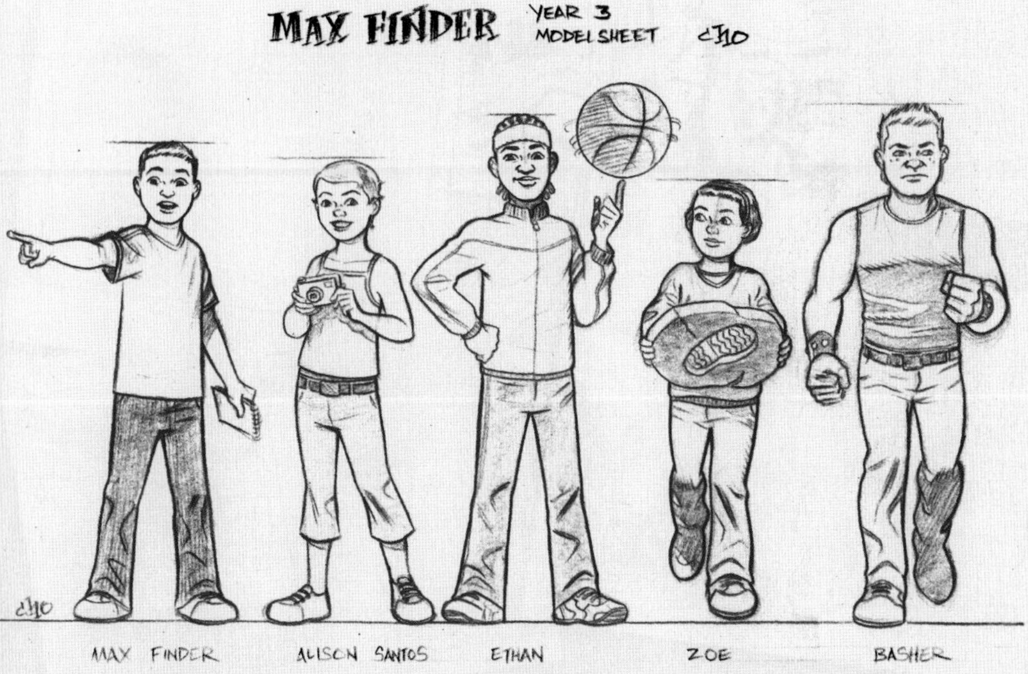
MAX FINDER
YEAR 3
MODEL SHEET
CHO
CHO
MAX FINDER
ALISON SANTOS
ETHAN
ZOE
BASHER

Making a Mystery

A *Max Finder Mystery* graphic story goes through many stages before it's published. Every case starts off with writer Liam O'Donnell creating a detailed script. Liam outlines the plot, writes the captions and dialogue, as well as describes what the characters and setting look like. Michael Cho, the comic artist, creates the illustrations from this script.

Storyboarding

First, Michael draws quick sketches called thumbnails and decides how the panels will work together to tell the story.

Drawing Rough Sketches

Using the sketches as guides, Michael creates the illustrations for the story in blue pencil.

Revising Roughs

Sometimes the comic editor requests changes to the panels.

Making a Mystery

Inking the Drawings

The illustrator draws the final artwork in black waterproof ink over the blue pencil drawings.

EDITOR'S NOTE:
MICHAEL'S JOB IS JUST ABOUT FINISHED. THE COMIC IS REALLY COMING TOGETHER.

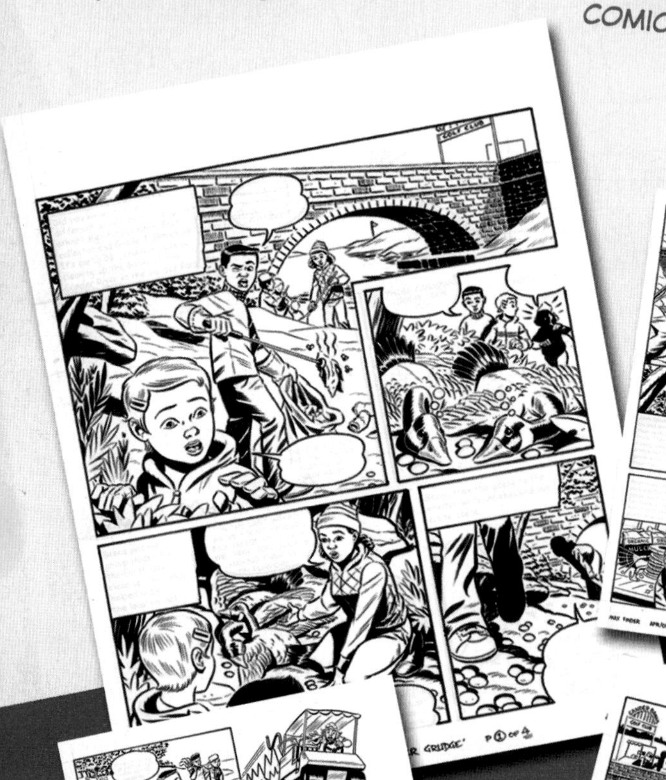

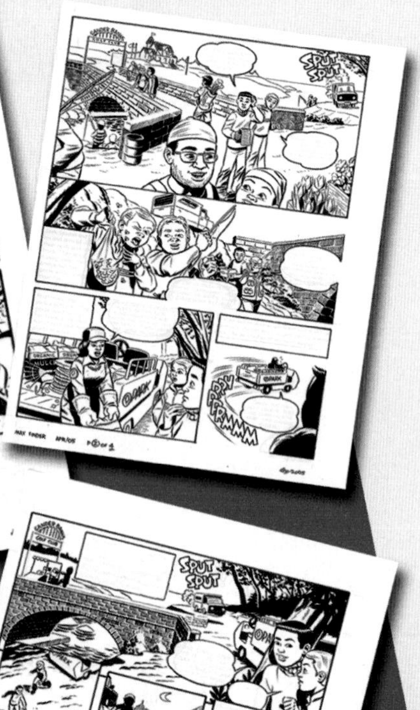
SPUT SPUT

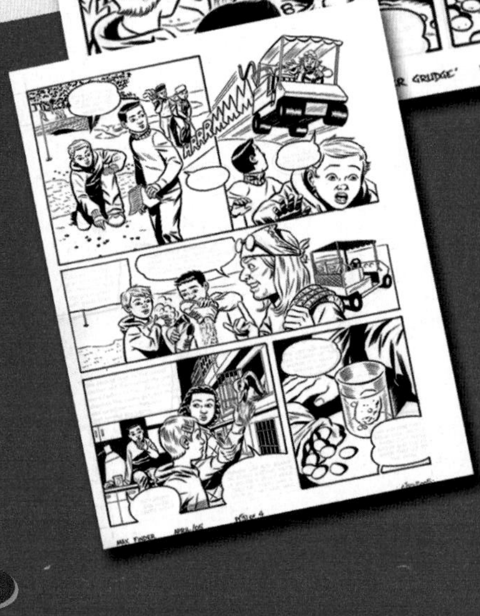

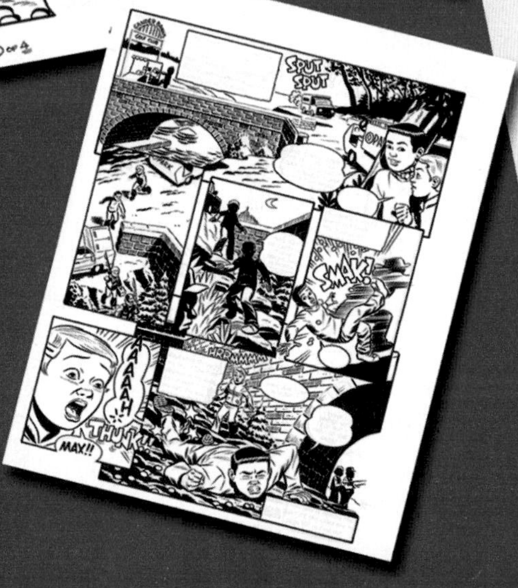
SPUT SPUT
SMAK!
AAAAAH!
THUNK!
MAX!!

Colouring the Art

Michael gives guidelines for colouring to a colourist, an artist who specializes in colouring comics on the computer.

Publishing the Comic

After a designer adds the edited story onto the coloured art, the mystery is ready to be published.

EDITOR'S NOTE: NEXT STOP FOR THE COMIC? YOUR COLLECTED CASEBOOK!

The Many Faces of Max

MAX FINDER

Liam O'Donnell

Liam O'Donnell approached *OWL Magazine* in 2002 with his idea for an interactive graphic mystery story — and *Max Finder Mystery* was born. Liam is the author of over twenty children's books including picture books, non-fiction titles, and graphic novels. He frequently writes about literacy and education for national magazines, and can be found online at www.liamodonnell.com.

Michael Cho

Michael Cho was born in Seoul, South Korea, and moved to Canada when he was six years old. A graduate of the Ontario College of Art and Design, his distinctive drawings and comics have appeared in magazines across North America and he has illustrated several children's books, including *Media Madness: An Insider's Guide to Media*. He is currently devoting his time to writing and drawing more comics, and you can always see his latest work online at www.michaelcho.com.

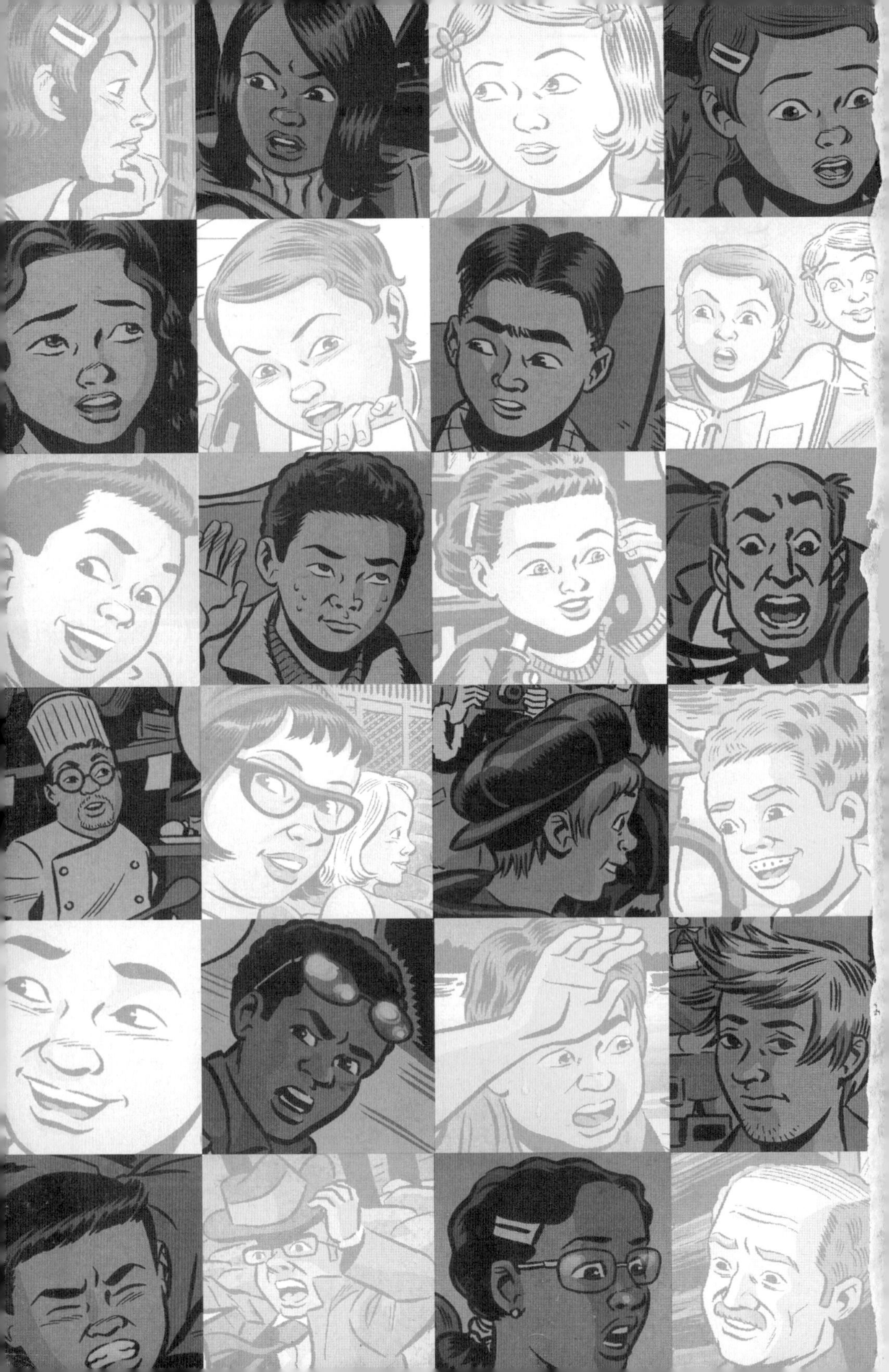